Stacks

Other publications by Caithness writers

Caithness Crime

Beyond the Mist

Flights of Imagination

Email Caithnesswriters@aol.com
Web site www.caithnesswriters.com

Published by
Overtheord Publishing
8-10 Louisburgh Street
Wick KW1 4BY

Artwork by

John Knowles
'The Stacks of Duncansby'

A collection of poems and stories, written, edited, proof-read,
designed and published by members of Caithness Writers.

Caithness Writers

Encourages members as creative individuals
Explores the craft of writing
Celebrates writers and writing in Caithness

.

Stacks

An Anthology

by

Caithness Writers

Contents

Stacks

Sharon Gunason Pottinger

We are the last defenders of the ancient coast
softer stones surrendered to the sea and the wind
seduced by a wave or battered in a storm
while we held fast.

Surrounded by the sea lapping at our feet
lonely bastions of a time before the water had salt
nursemaid to sea birds
we hold fast.

Welcome to Wick

Catherine M. Byrne

Laura adjusted her bag, not that it was heavy. Sad really, that after fifteen years all her earthly belongings could be stored in one rucksack. The apprehension had begun in Queen Street station, Glasgow, and had grown with every mile. Now she felt physically sick. She looked around. Bittersweet memories that had shifted like shadows with every passing mile grew stronger. In the distance she could hear bagpipes, a slow mournful dirge. It was funny how a sound, once taken for granted, could stir the soul when not heard for many years.

Turning, she looked back at the sign she had not been able to see from the train, but had known was there. Above the entrance to the station, where it always had been.

WELCOME TO WICK.

But there would be no welcome for her. 'Let them go to hell,' she said aloud, her voice sounding foreign in the music of the birds and the traffic.

She chose to take the path by the river, the path where she had run and played as a child, the path where she and Stephen had walked hand in hand, so in love. At least, *she* had been in love. Back then, she believed he had been, too.

Above her the crows argued and complained, trees swayed slightly, leaves rustling against each other, all gossiping, she thought with a wry smile, imagining the conversation.

'Is that Laura Parker?'

'My God, it is. Hasn't she aged. Wasn't it her who...'

'Shameless hussy, showing her face back here again.'

'The very nerve.'

She almost laughed out loud. It was what the majority of people of this small town would say once they heard of her return. At least those who knew her – or knew of her.

The sun fell in dappled pebbles at her feet and sparkled on the surface of the water. Nothing much had changed by the riverbank. The trees had grown higher, there were no longer rowing boats tied up on the jetty across the water, and where there had been a caravan park, there was now a garden. The church still stood where it had for centuries, poking its great spire through the greenery. The church where she and Stephen had taken their wedding vows. She had been happy that day, so full of hope for the future. Back then, she'd thought it was the best day of her life, that and the birth of her daughter, two years later.

Liar, liar, she silently shouted at the ghost of her twenty-four year old self as she visualised the long-ago scene. Her in virginal white, he in full highland regalia. And he had looked so handsome. As she gazed at him, her heart had been full of love.

Her parents were there. Mother in pink, father in navy blue. She diverted her thoughts. Sadly her mother had passed away in the intervening years and her father had moved abroad with a new woman without telling her.

She passed the statue of John Calder, historian of Caithness, the old milk marketing board now in ruins, and the hill where a cannon once stood pointing up river. She briefly wondered where it had gone. The wooden bridge was still there though, the bridge that would take her across the water to the place she once called home.

With every step her heartbeat quickened, and by the time she saw him it had become a gallop. He was where he said he would be. Steady, predictable Stephen, standing beneath the hill. In spite of the stoop of shoulders that seemed to carry a great weight, and the absence of hair that had once been thick and black, she recognised the proud, straight nose, the curve of the cheek, softer now, the blunt short fingers on hands that hung by his side. He was staring across the water towards the church and it flashed through her mind that perhaps, he too, was remembering their wedding day.

She took a deep, unsteady breath, tried to swallow though her mouth was dry, walked towards him and stopped. Her fingers clenched around the strap of her bag as she waited until he sensed her presence and turned his head. He did not speak, merely stared as though not quite seeing her, as though she was a wraith formed from the haar that would drift up river when the sun had sunk.

'Aren't you going to say hello?' she asked softly.

'Laura. You look...'

My God, don't say he was going to tell her she looked good. 'Like shit?' She finished the sentence for him.

'No...no, I...' He lowered his eyes. 'Why did you come back? I told you when you phoned. You're dead to us.'

'Yet you came here to meet me. Today.'

'I was afraid you'd come to the house otherwise − like you threatened.'

'Why afraid? I'm not going to hurt anyone.'

'No?' He gave a short, derogatory laugh. 'I told you how our daughter was; she has everything she needs. Why disrupt her life?'

'Oh yes, you told me she's going to university after the summer. Art and design isn't it? You think telling me's enough? I want to see her.'

'We've arranged a party for her tonight. Don't ruin it. She's forgotten you. What more do you need to know? Go back on the next train − back to where you belong.'

4

She stepped closer, so that she stood directly in front of him. 'I don't belong there. I never did.'

He straightened his shoulders, looked down at her and he rubbed his face. The stubble on his chin rasped. When had he changed, stopped caring? He had always been so immaculate, so clean-shaven.

His voice rose. 'You destroyed me – destroyed us all. Please don't destroy our child.'

'I've paid. I've paid with fifteen years of my life. Have you any idea what that was like?' She would not cry. The tears had been frozen inside her many years ago.

'For God's sake, you killed a man.'

'And I've paid dearly for it. Just let me see Amy.'

'She doesn't want to see you.'

Laura closed her eyes against the pain. *Liar, liar,* the words circled in her head.

'What have you told her? What have you said?' This was not how it was meant to unfold.

'I haven't told her the truth, if that's what you're afraid of.' He sighed. His eyes were heavy, dark ringed.

'I'm not afraid.' It suddenly dawned on her that perhaps it was he who was afraid of the truth and that was the real reason he wanted her to stay away. 'So you're still living a lie?'

'It's for her sake.'

'You loved me once. At least you *said* you did, but we both know that wasn't true, don't we?'

'I thought I knew you once.'

'And I thought I knew you.'

Stephen had the grace to look ashamed. Up river, the slash of crimson split the horizon.

Laura batted the air. With the lowering of the sun, the midges filled the space around her and nipped her hands and face.

'Amy's happy. I will not let you spoil it.' His voice was sharp with the ring of finality.

What had she expected? That he would agree to her demands, that somewhere inside he would remember the happy times, remember what a good mother she had been, forgive her?

He fumbled in his pocket and brought out an envelope, opened the flap and showed her the wad of notes inside. 'Take this and go.' He thrust the package at her. 'Go to a hotel. Stay the night and be on the six-twenty train out of here tomorrow morning.'

With him towering above her she felt intimidated, vulnerable. Without moving to take the money, she tilted her chin upwards and her narrowed eyes met Stephen's. At that moment he reminded her of the midges. As if he, too, wanted to suck the life-blood from her.

'What does Amy know? What does she believe?' she said.

He opened his mouth to speak and at the same time his eyes left hers and settled on something beyond and behind her. His voice stopped as if it had caught behind his teeth and filled his mouth so that he could not close it. His Adam's apple bobbed as he swallowed the words he had to say. Then they came from him like a hiss. 'Oh, my God, no.' He stuffed the money back into his pocket.

Laura spun around, followed his line of vision and saw a young girl marching across the bridge. She saw narrow, denim-clad hips and white cropped hair tipped with pink, the determined swing of the arms, and she knew.

Her heart swelled as the girl came towards them, the eyes which were fixed on Laura's radiating a cold fury. Laura knew then that the recognition had been mutual, that something in the genes had called to genes, that blood had called to blood. And at that moment, in this child, she recognised her own rebellious nature, her own deep-rooted sense of pain.

'Amy,' said Laura, the name coming in a breath of air, trembling from her heart. She drank in the smooth skin, the dark arched eyebrows, the slight upward turn of the nose, the stubborn set of the chin, the lips now curled with anger. And the piercings; ears, nose, lip, and she saw herself all those years ago. Dyed hair, pierced skin, that was good. Stephen was allowing her to be her own person. Had her parents allowed her the same freedom, perhaps the anger would not have bottled up inside her, swelling until it could no longer be contained.

Stephen moved forward and stretched his hand towards his daughter as if to stop her, but she side-stepped and his fingers remained in the air.

'What are you doing here?' he shouted.

'I knew there was something up. Silences whenever I came in the room. You know granny can never keep a secret, especially from me.' Amy breathed in so quickly her nostrils quivered and she fixed her furious glare on her father. 'She didn't want to tell me, but I got it out of her. You didn't want me to know. Why?'

'Amy...you...you're beautiful. Won't you leave us, Stephen?' Laura said softly, 'Now that she's here, won't you let us talk?'

'What is there to talk about?' Amy turned to face her mother, her small fists bunched at her sides, arms slightly bent as if she were ready to strike. All the fury her eyes had fired at her father she now directed at Laura.

Laura took a step towards her, but the girl backed away.

'Don't come near me,' she hissed.

'Oh, darling, I always meant to come back.'

'And you waited fifteen years?'

'There are things you obviously don't know.'

'I know that my mother abandoned me when I was three years old. I know that she's not welcome in my life now.' She spun to face Stephen again. 'You should never have agreed to meet her, and...and gone behind my back.' She pointed her finger at Laura. 'Why did she *have* to come back? Why? We were doing just fine without her.' She took a shuddering breath.

'I'm sorry, pet. I was trying to protect you.'

'I'm eighteen today, Dad. I don't need protecting.'

Desperate to make some amends, to draw the girl towards her, Laura reached down and picked up her rucksack. 'I've brought something for you, I've...' she fumbled with the catch.

'I want nothing from *you*!' said Amy. She spat the words out, then bit her lip which had begun to tremble.

'Now do you see – do you understand?' asked Stephen. 'You heard her. Please go.'

A couple with a dog passed by, turned their heads to look, and on meeting Laura's glare, glanced away and hurried on.

Heart hammering, Laura sucked air through her teeth and lowered her voice. 'I just want to talk, just to talk, tell you...'

'No, don't say another word,' Stephen held up a hand as if in a plea for mercy.

'Tell me what?' Amy said, quieter now. 'That you couldn't love me enough to stay with me? I waited for you. I cried so much. It's too late. I don't need you now.'

They stood shoulder to shoulder, father and daughter, facing Laura, united in their rejection of her.

'You should have told her the truth.' Laura said to Stephen. 'Everything.'

'Just go,' Stephen's voice shook. A bead of sweat ran down his cheek.

'What are you afraid of, Stephen?'

'You, ruining everything again.'

'Then I'll tell her,' said Laura, not knowing how much she intended to say.

'Tell me what?' Amy stared at her mother, a stare that was no longer defiant, as if the mask had slipped and revealed the frightened child underneath.

'That I didn't *want* to leave you. Didn't you get the letters I sent?'

'The letters?'

'You didn't get them, did you?'

'Daddy?'

Stephen met Laura's eyes and shook his head, recrimination in every line of his face.

'Why...why?' Amy looked from one to the other and her voice rose. 'Somebody tell me what's going on.'

Laura swallowed. 'I've been in prison.'

Amy's eyes opened in disbelief. 'For... for what?'

'Look, let's just go home. I'll explain everything. I promise.' Stephen grabbed Amy's arm and tried to lead her away, but she tore herself out of his grip.

'I want to hear what *she* has to say.'

Laura swallowed. She'd gone this far. She licked dry lips. 'For murder.'

The air hushed between them. Even the gulls appeared to hold their pathetic crying, a barking dog fell silent, all mute in a frozen moment. The fight seemed to have gone from Stephen and he stared at her with a desperate despondency in his eyes. Laura almost felt sorry for him.

Amy turned incredulous eyes towards her father. 'What...what's she saying, Daddy?'

He glared at Laura and pointed up the slope towards the railway line. 'Go back,' he hissed, 'Go away and leave us alone. I never told her for her sake. I never told anyone, for her sake.'

As if she couldn't bear the pain, Amy fell onto her knees. 'When I was six,' she said in a whisper, 'I came home from school crying because someone said my mother was a murderer.' She looked up at her father. 'You told me it was lies and I trusted you. I spent years fighting, getting into trouble for a lie.'

'Come and sit on the seat, the ground'll be damp,' said Laura reaching out.

'Huh, motherly concern,' said Amy, her face hard, the mask back in place. 'How touching.' She rose from the ground. Damp patches circled her knees. She turned and walked a few steps, then spun round to face her mother again.

'Who did you kill?'

Laura looked at Stephen and her lips parted.

Stephen shook his head, his eyes piteous. Another bead of sweat trickled down his forehead. His skin had turned a pasty, unhealthy colour, his breath turned into quick laboured gasps. He rifled in his pocket.

'Are you all right, Daddy?' Amy reached towards him, suddenly all concern.

Stephen found what he'd been looking for. Raising the small red bottle, he depressed the nozzle and sprayed something into his mouth. 'I'll be…okay…now,' he said.

Laura saw the girl's fear, sensed the warmth between the man and child, felt the pang of jealousy and regret for the wasted years. What had she imagined? That she could somehow recapture the lost time? Find a bond that had been broken so long ago? Who was she kidding? Amy would never look at *her* that way.

'He's got a bad heart,' said Amy, as if she needed to explain her change in demeanour. She narrowed her eyes. 'If he has another attack it'll be your fault. Now tell me, who did you kill?'

Laura took stock of Stephen's pallor. 'A friend, who was no friend at all,' she said at last.

'I don't understand.' Amy shook her head.

'No one does.'

'Laura, please...' The words were wrenched from Stephen as if the agony inside would not let them go.

'It doesn't matter now,' she said, putting an end to his pain. 'All I wanted was to see Amy again. Make sure she was okay. I'll leave now.'

'Tell me what happened. An explanation's the least you owe me.' The coldness was back in the girl's eyes, was back for Laura.

'I had a temper, still have. I didn't mean to kill anyone. I saw the red mist and grabbed the first thing to hand. It's over. I've done my time.' She closed her eyes and ears against the vision of the heavy glass ashtray splitting in two, its sharp edges slicing skin and artery, the crunch of bone. Her own high-pitched scream. And the blood, she never knew one body could hold so much blood. She hadn't faced the image in years.

Locked it away in the cupboard of her mind and thrown away the key.

'But...why?' asked Amy.

'He upset me, that was all. Ask your father – I'm sure he has all the answers.'

'I can't believe this. You mean you killed someone because he pissed you off?'

'I guess so. Told you, I had a temper. I'm not proud of it.' *Liar, liar*, shouted the voice in her head.

Amy turned away, walked across the green, sat on a swing and, with her head hanging, she slowly pushed herself to and fro.

'Thank you,' said Stephen, wiping his brow. His colour was returning.

'Don't you dare thank me. If I say nothing it's for her sake not yours.'

She held out her hand. 'Give me the price of a B & B. I'll be on the morning train. I've a probation officer to see in a couple of days anyhow.'

He handed her the envelope with the notes. 'There's five hundred there, enough to see you alright, well a bit better than, you know, whatever you're getting.'

'Thank you.' Tears stung behind her eyes. 'You've made a good job of bringing up our daughter. I'm pleased about that at least.' Laura turned to go.

'Just tell me one thing,' Stephen said.

She stopped and waited.

'Why him and not me?'

Laura smiled, turned to face him and studied his expression. She wanted to see it change. Wanted to see pain.

'I was in love with *him*.'

A look of shocked horror replaced the relief on Stephen's face. It was a small triumph.

She walked to the top of the hill where she used to play on the old cannon that was no longer there.

He didn't try to stop her. She looked back to where Amy still sat on the swing, her head hanging. No. She couldn't tell her what really happened. Just seeing her daughter might not have been all she wanted, but knowing how she had turned out, how close she was to her father, it was the best she could hope to get. Maybe one day in her more mature years, Amy would come looking for her.

In the meantime she would write, yes that's what she'd do. Write a letter every week. Probably they'd all go in the bin, but at least she'd know she tried. And in the end there was nothing else she could have done.

Yes, she had wanted to tell the truth, considered it. But how could she shatter the illusion this child had of her father? How could she tell her that she had found Stephen in bed with the best man at their wedding, his best friend? The same friend who had held *her* hand, the same friend *she* had confided in as her marriage bounced from rock to rock and eventually crumbled. The same friend who had kissed away *her* tears, became *her* lover. Had it been anyone else, she might have shut the door, walked away from that marriage, that life. She might have felt relief, at last knowing that the reason for Stephen's indifference had nothing to do with her. They might have even remained friends. But what was the point on reflecting what might have been?

'Happy birthday, darling,' she whispered to the forlorn figure on the swing at the bottom of the hill, although she knew Amy could not hear. She waited a beat, hoping the girl would look up, meet her eyes, reconsider, give her a chance, but it was not to be.

As she trailed along the path, she allowed her mind to take her back into the past. She had been vulnerable, felt unloved. She should have known then that there was something wrong, but she had blamed herself. And *he* was there, handsome, charming, with a ready smile, and time, yes, he's always had time for her. At first his friendship was all she wanted, someone who could see the situation for himself. When had it turned to love? She didn't know. Perhaps when he told her how much he'd always admired her, when he told her how Stephen didn't deserve her, or when he pulled her into his arms and whispered the endearments she longed to hear.

Liar, liar.

How could he have betrayed her trust, shattered her heart the way he did?

She passed the sign above the entrance to the station.

After tomorrow, she would never see that sign again. She adjusted her backpack and marched along the path, tears running freely down her face.

Suddenly, she heard a sound behind her, the light running of feet, a breathy sigh, and then a voice. 'Mother,' one word.

She spun round and Amy stood there, teeth trapping her bottom lip, her eyes like pools. 'You must have had good reason. Maybe one day...' Amy blinked quickly then wiped her cheeks.

'Yes, maybe one day I'll tell you.' But Laura knew she never would.

'Will you write – phone?'

'Of course I will.' Laura counted each breath.

Amy walked towards her, then stopped, just a heartbeat away.

Laura opened her arms.

Amy shook her head. 'It's too soon.'

'I understand.'

Laura allowed her arms to drop to her side.

'I...I thought you might want this.' Amy handed her a slip of paper. 'My mobile number.' Then she turned and was gone, running away, swallowed up by the vegetation and the gathering haar.

'Amy...I love you.' Laura shouted. Her heart swelled with the adrenaline of hope, the promise of a future, of one day connecting once more with her child, her baby. She tilted her head backwards, stared at the pale sky above the treetops and, driven by adrenaline fuelled hope, spun around.

When she stopped spinning the first thing she saw was the sign above the railway station.

WELCOME TO WICK.

Now the words held more meaning than they'd ever had before.

Read more by Catherine
www.catherinebyrne-author.com

Guess Who Came to Dinner

Moira Dearness

Why did I do it; why did I let my friends talk me into it? After tonight they'll probably be my ex-friends!

'Forget that rat, Denise. You need to move on,' they said.

'Find new interests; do something you've never done before.'

Well, this is certainly something I've never done before, and I won't be doing it again!

The rat that I'm supposed to forget is my ex, Jack. We'd been together for nine years, and had planned the wedding. Mind you, it was me who did all the planning. I put his reluctance to do anything down to being male and laziness. I should've read the signs. A year ago I came home after working late to find the female equivalent of a "Dear John" taped to the computer. At least it was a letter and not a text.

He couldn't go through with it, he said. Better to end it now before we married. He'd already arranged a transfer and was moving away. I was gutted and blamed myself. Perhaps I should have left things as they were and not pushed him into getting married.

A few days after he left, someone told me he'd moved in with some woman he'd met while away on a course a few weeks earlier and that she was no chicken. I might have understood if he'd fallen for someone younger – he was coming up to forty and I wasn't far behind, but it was a slap in the face that he preferred somebody older than me.

So I was shoved into applying for that awful TV show, "Come Dine with Me". I've always thought that people who took part in reality TV shows were a bunch of sad attention-seekers. But now here I am, the first host of the week, waiting for my guests to arrive, nerves in tatters having spent the day with my every move recorded by the TV cameras. How sad is that?

I'm no cook. My "signature dish" is beans on toast, made special with a covering of bubbling, melted Cheddar. I can't see that impressing anyone. Now and again I've watched the show and wondered if, when they view the playback on television, the contestants cringe when they see what they're like.

Some of them are so disorganized and only start preparation while their guests are making awkward conversation in the sitting room and drinking cocktails that look like anti-freeze. Others just don't seem to have a clue as to what should be done first and waste so much time before starting to cook. The menus some of them dream up are bizarre; the worst I've seen is the Scottish millionaire who served pig's trotters, because his granny used to cook them for him. You also get the cheats who get friends or the local restaurant to cook for them and, I must admit, I was thinking along those lines myself.

Trying to decide on the menu was a nightmare and Delia Smith was no inspiration. What the hell; I'll just give them my favourites, but not steak. One man's rare is another's not cooked properly. Thank goodness there aren't any vegetarians. They always seem to hate the stuffed peppers, courgettes or mushrooms, or else hosts commit the sin of not using vegetable stock for the soup.

The other thing that raised my blood pressure was knowing the guests would snoop around the house, even opening the drawers in the bedroom. I would die if they opened my knickers drawer; I was tempted to rush out and buy some lacy thongs to replace the off-white passion killers that I usually wear. Getting my house in a fit state would have needed the combined efforts of "Kim and Aggie" and "60-Minute Makeover", although in my case it would be a sixty-hour makeover!

Anyhow, I am now ready and waiting for my guests to arrive. The house is reasonably clean and tidy. Food is prepared; parsnip soup just needs heating up, pork and mushroom casserole is simmering in the oven, brioche bread and butter pudding made and Bailey's ice cream in the freezer. Six bottles of supermarket plonk are chilling and champagne is in the ice bucket.

I just hope all my guests get on. Producers seem to choose people who are so different there's bound to be conflict. I'll soon find out. There's the doorbell. A very handsome older man, looking remarkably like George Clooney, is on the doorstep, clutching an enormous bouquet. We exchange names. I hope I remember that he is Barry and don't call him George. I let him kiss me on the cheek. I hate this kissing the air and making silly 'mwah' noises.

Not far behind him is thirty-something Wayne, who is casually and comfortably dressed, then Sherrie: very young, very blonde and dressed to impress. Both of them give me red wine, which makes me wonder if I've made a mistake in buying only white. In the sitting room I ask Barry to open the champagne. I'm shaking so much I daren't try.

Everything is very pleasant and going very well when the final guest arrives. A very tall woman, looking and dressed like Mama Cass, sails into the house, tells me she is Julie and nearly smothers me with a hug. In the sitting room she also hugs everyone and very soon takes over the conversation.

I serve the starter straightaway, giving them no time to go upstairs. As soon as they finish the soup, I dish up the casserole. Julie tells us she is only living and working in this town temporarily and that her partner used to live here. They met in her home town on a business course. I'm beginning to feel uneasy. She leaves nothing out, tells us he had been with someone for years and was bored and wanted out. She says Jack and she were made for each other. She calls him her "toy boy" – he is a bit younger than her. By now I've got a very strong feeling that this is the woman Jack left me for.

I say to her, 'Aren't you worried he'll leave you after a few years?'

'No way,' she says. '*I* know how to keep a man. I won't be pestering him to get married.'

That did it! I just couldn't resist it, so when she stops talking to take a mouthful I say casually, 'Julie, I think I know Jack. He's got a most unusual tattoo in a very odd place, hasn't he?'

It wasn't choking on a piece of pork that shut her up for the rest of the meal. She left soon afterwards with a lame excuse about a migraine. I wonder which one of us will be first to pull out of this contest!

Imagine

Meg Macleod

imagine
when you breathe
the places the air has visited

it has travelled the oceans
touched the highest mountains
drifted along close cropped straths
across plains and high sierras
it has lingered in redwood forests
gathering the resin scent of centuries
and tumbled with glaciers
into the cold home of Beluga whales

invisible harvester of the past
carrying the last cries of wounded soldiers
exhaled in the first of new-born babes

imagine
when you breath
who breathed before you
and who will take your breath onwards

if words could fasten your thoughts
onto the pages of rock
if there was the slightest chance

in the distant tomorrow
someone somewhere
might breathe them in
you would speak them wouldn`t you
you would breathe them out into the air
you would shout them
wouldn`t you?
sing them
wouldn't you?
you would want them to know
the sunrise and sunset of this arching sky
the first snowdrop
and the blackbird
you heard yesterday
distilling the world into music

you would be a poet
wouldn`t you?

Read more by Meg
https://www.amazon.co.uk/Raven-Songs-Meg-Macleod

Unlocking the Past

Morag MacRae

'Where are you going, Mum?' asked Sally, shivering in the cold draught whistling through the open front door.

'To meet Doris for coffee. I always meet Doris on Tuesdays.'

'But this is Wednesday, Mum. Besides Doris...' she stopped. She couldn't bring herself to remind her that Doris was gone. Every time she did, it was as though her mother was hearing the news for the first time.

'Doris?' she sounded puzzled and Sally could see the confusion in her eyes. She couldn't do it.

'Doris will be waiting,' said Sally. 'Let me help you down the steps.'

She grabbed her coat, pulled it on quickly and took her mother's arm. Once at the bottom, her mother waved her hand in dismissal.

'I'm fine now. Off you go.'

Sally turned and looked back when she reached the door. 'No, that's the wrong way,' she groaned.

The direction her mother had taken led out of town. As usual Sally followed at a safe distance. She was puzzled as to why her mother had changed direction. She had always headed into town, sat in a café waiting to meet Doris and when she didn't appear, she returned home.

She quickened her pace when she saw her mother arrive at a crossing. This had never been an obstacle when she had gone in the other direction. Her mother joined the people already waiting to cross and Sally stood behind her. Without warning, her mother moved forward. Sally grabbed her shoulders and pulled her back to safety.

'Leave me alone!' her mother shouted as she pummelled Sally with her fists. She was shocked. Her mother had never been violent before. She could feel the eyes of the other people penetrating her anxiety-drenched body. She's my mother and she's got dementia, Sally wanted to scream at them. A middle-aged man walked over.

'What's her name?' he asked Sally.

'Annie. Why?'

The man turned to Sally's mother, crooked his arm and said, 'May I escort you across the road, Annie?'

Sally stood in disbelief as her mother slipped her arm into his. When the green man appeared, they walked safely over. Sally thought she could hear them singing. She hurried to catch up and sure enough the strains of 'We'll Meet Again' drifted back to her. Once they were across, her mother slid her arm out and carried on along the pavement.

'Who *are* you?' Sally asked the man.

'I've been there with my own mother. It's a very difficult time. Singing the old songs is good therapy for you both. Somehow they know all the words and you'll find it's a release of tension for you, too.'

'Thanks for that,' said Sally. 'I'd better catch her up.'

'Wait,' said the man as he pulled a card from his pocket. 'Call me if you ever need someone to talk to.'

'Thank you.' Sally accepted the card. 'But I'm sure I'll be fine.'

She hurried to catch up with her mother, who had entered a café. Sally sat at a table nearby and ordered a latte. She watched as the waiter brought two cups of coffee to her mother's table. She felt a strong urge to go over and tell her Doris wouldn't be coming. Doris would never be coming to join her for coffee again. Tears ran down Sally's cheeks. She felt frustrated at not being able to communicate with this person she loved so much. Maybe the stranger was right. She needed someone to talk to. Her thoughts were interrupted by a scream from another customer in the café. A waiter had tripped and poured a pot of hot water over a boy's hands. Before she knew it, her mother raced over.

'I'm a nurse,' she said. 'Go and bring a bowl of cold water.'

The waiter quickly returned with the bowl.

'Now put your hands in this,' she said. 'It'll sting a bit but keep them there.'

The boy duly obeyed. Sally watched her mother stroke the boy's head as he grimaced with the pain.

'Well done, son,' she said. 'Has the pain gone?'

The boy nodded.

'Waiter, bring damp cloths, please,' said her mother. 'Your mummy will wrap your hands in the cloths and that will help to keep the pain away.'

The boy nodded again.

She directed her next order to the boy's mother. 'Take him to the hospital, but I think the cold water will have prevented blistering.'

'Thank you so much,' said the boy's mother.

Sally could not believe what she had just seen. It was yet another memory from her mother's past. Could the past be the answer?

The incident over, her mother left the café. All thought of Doris had vanished. Sally felt relieved when she walked outside and saw her mother heading back the way she had come. Once inside the house, there was no conversation about the day's events. No conversation at all. Always the ominous silence as if Sally didn't exist. She extricated the stranger's card from her pocket and dialled the number.

'Mr. Greyson, I'm the woman you gave your card to at the crossing on Shepherd Street. You helped my mother, Annie, across the road,' said Sally.

'Please call me Tom. I'm glad you called. I guess you need someone to talk to?'

They arranged to meet the following day. She dialled the relief carer and asked her to sit with her mother while she was out. When she arrived at the rendezvous, a nearby café, Tom was already there. She sat down at the table.

'How can I help?' he asked.

Sally related the events from the previous day. 'I get the feeling people like Mum remember things from their past. That's what I wanted to speak to you about.'

'I can help you there, but I'd prefer to know a little more about your life with your mother from the beginning,' said Tom.

Sally found it therapeutic to unburden herself of everything that had occurred since her mother had been diagnosed three years previously. Tom sat quietly sipping his coffee. He didn't speak until she finished.

'Three years is a long time. I think you've been marvellous. I only lasted one and a half before I couldn't cope anymore. My mother's now in residential care.'

'Residential care! I'm sorry, Tom, but Mum isn't going into care.'

'No, Sally, I wasn't suggesting that. My mother's in a wonderful environment. I was thinking more of you visiting the home and finding ways of reaching your mother. I'm going to visit tomorrow. Would you like to come with me?'

'I'd love to,' said Sally.

The following afternoon they visited the home. Sally was shown around by one of the staff. Some of the residents were sleeping peacefully in armchairs. Two women were baking in the kitchen.

'They were cooks when they were young. They know the ingredients without a recipe book,' said the carer. 'Through here is where various activities take place.'

Sally saw people painting on easels. Others were knitting, crocheting or working on tapestries. Two men were hammering nails into a piece of wood.

'Come out into the garden,' said the carer.

Sally stood in the sunshine watching a man painting the garden shed. He looked contented.

'Tom's painted that shed three times in the last six months but he's happy. That's what matters. Look there's more of the residents tending the garden. We grow all our vegetables here. Loads of flowers in the house in the summer.'

'You're doing marvellous work,' said Sally. 'I'd no idea what to expect.'

'Don't get the wrong idea. Not all homes for people with dementia are like this. It takes time and dedication,' said the carer. 'I'll leave you now to take a wander round.'

Sally walked back inside and saw Tom sitting with his mother. She was stroking a grey cat on her lap. They were singing quietly until a few of the other residents joined in. The singing grew louder. The room quickly reverberated with the strains of, 'It's A Long Way To Tipperary.'

Sally joined in. She looked over at Tom and smiled. A man rose from his armchair and rushed to the piano. Many more songs were sung with gusto until Tom gripped Sally's elbow. 'We need to be going now. It'll soon be time for their meal.'

On the journey back, Sally said, 'That was a real eye-opener. What a marvellous place! The carers reached into each resident's past. Mum was a midwife before she married.'

'That gives you a starting point. Buy some dolls and see what she does with them,' said Tom.

'I'll give it a try,' said Sally.

'Phone me if you get a result.'

She felt elated. Tom had given her hope.

The next day she set off to the nearest toyshop and bought a doll that cried plus a cradle. When she arrived home, she set it in the kitchen and called her mother through for lunch. When the meal was over, Sally discretely pressed the doll's stomach.

It wailed. Her mother spun round, walked over to the cradle and lifted the doll. She stood dumbfounded as she heard her mother crooning over it. For the rest of the day, her mother tended and cared for the doll. She appeared brighter and more alert. This was a turning point for Sally. She dialled Tom's number.

'It's unbelievable, Tom,' she said. 'Mum's come alive. She's doted on that doll all day. It's been wonderful. Thank you so much.'

'You do know…'

'Yes, I do know. There will come a time when I won't be able to cope at home. I understand. That day, when I first met you, I thought it *was* that time but you've given me longer and I'm grateful.'

Weeks passed. Enjoyable weeks for Sally as she watched her mother tend to more dolls. She also bought a kitten that had become a real treat for, not just her mother, but Sally as well. Tom had become Sally's confidant. Someone she trusted and listened to. Then came the day her mother, for no apparent reason, became extremely violent. Sally dialled Tom's number.

'I tried to get Mum up this morning and she lashed out at me and called me names.' Sally began to cry.

'Sally, listen to me. My mother was like that. Always remember it's the dementia, not you. Maybe it's time.'

'But, Tom, I feel so guilty.'

'I did, too. I felt I'd failed my mother but, Sally, you've done wonders for yours. You've done more than I did. Why don't I contact the care home my mother's in and see if there's a vacancy?'

'That's very kind of you.'

Two weeks later, Sally bundled a suitcase into Tom's car. 'Mum, we're going on a holiday.'

'That's nice,' said her mother. 'I like holidays. Are we staying in a hotel?'

'Yes, we're staying in a lovely hotel.'

As they journeyed to the care home, Sally sat in the back holding her mother's hand. Tears ran down her cheeks as they sang, 'We'll Meet Again'. She met Tom's eyes in the mirror and knew what the future held for her. Joint visits to the care home and a strong shoulder to cry on afterwards.

Read more by Morag
www.moragmacrae.co.uk

A Woman to Kill for

Rodger Bailey

Jack Finch leaned his short, fat body against the back of his seat, waved the waiter away and gave his new friend a wary look.

He had come across the snooty Carl Summerwest in Claridge's bar and his first instinct had been to lift his wallet. But, to his surprise, Summerwest had come on to him real friendly and a fellow New Yorker to boot. They migrated to the dining room, where they shot their mouths off over politics, music, the mayor's attempts to crack down on organised crime and compared the best restaurants that London and NYC had to offer.

For three days Jack contented himself with just taking the drinks and meals Summerwest had insisting on putting on his own tab and all the time, he now realised, the guy had been softening him up. Mousy Monahan would die laughing.

He folded his arms and gave Summerwest his disappointed scowl.

'What kind of favour, Carl?'

Summerwest gave a little smile, put the menu to one side, pressed manicured fingers together and gazed at him down his long, elegant nose.

'Heavens, don't look at me like that, Jack,' he said, rolling his eyes. 'I'm not going to ask you to kill someone!'

It wouldn't matter if he did, Jack thought, though it would cost more than a couple of Gordon Ramsay specials.

From a leather case, Summerwest produced a round silver locket on a chain. He pressed the catch and it flipped open. A coin tumbled onto the table.

'Take a look, Jack. It's just an ordinary silver shilling piece. The sort they stopped making years ago. All I want is for you to take this locket to an address near here, with a note enclosed, and bring back the reply.'

Jack picked up the coin with all the indifference he could muster and looked at the head.

'So whose kisser's this?'

'The young Queen Victoria's.'

Jack put the shilling on the table and pushed it back. With the possible exception of Mousy, he was nobody's gofer.

'Something wrong with the mail?'

Summerwest delicately replaced the coin in the locket and leaned forward.

'Discretion, Jack. Believe me, you would not entrust such a sensitive errand to the mail. Heavens, anyone might open it and ask questions of considerable awkwardness. And for me to take it in person could distress several people on whom I have no wish to impose that emotion. I have to find someone who can be relied on to put it into the right hands.' He nodded at Jack. 'And I'm a pretty good judge of character.'

Honeyed words will get you nowhere, Jack thought. He knocked back the rest of his drink in one go and felt the alcohol burning its way like acid into his resolve. Before he could blink, a fresh one appeared at his elbow.

'I don't know, Carl,' he said decisively, moving the glass with its golden contents so that it lay in front of him.

Summerwest pressed on eagerly.

'It'll take an hour. Tops. And tomorrow evening, if you're agreeable, I have tickets for a concert. And afterwards,' he added with a little smile, 'we can eat at Le Gavroche. You'll love it.'

The softening up, the sweet talk, now the bribe. Jack thought Summerwest would make a great Congressman. Just the mention of Le Gavroche put a strain on his waistband. He figured the concert would be just a load of tuxed-up guys forming a tribute band to long dead composers. Not exactly Alicia Keys, but it could be endured. He took another swallow.

'Whose are the right hands?' He glared at his glass accusingly.

'Her name is Francesca Barrington-MacNeil.'

There was silence. Jack wrapped his knuckles on the table.

'Tell me more, Carl. I don't do blind dates.'

Summerwest hesitated, fiddling with his napkin and straightening his knife and fork before replying with his usual hauteur.

'It's personal, Jack. *Very* personal. Need to know only, I'm afraid.'

'Where dames are concerned, *I* need to know,' Jack countered. 'Don't play me for a schnook! Tell me what's going on or it's no deal.'

Summerwest drummed his fingers on the table. 'Very well, if you insist on pressing me. When I was eighteen, my parents took me on vacation to Europe. While in London we went to a concert where I met Francesca Brownlee, as she was then. She was with her parents in the box next to ours and as crazy about music as I was. We were instantly smitten and for two whole wonderful months we were so happy as we dreamed of our coming life together. After returning home, I wrote and wrote but got no reply. Nor could I get through on the phone. I was going frantic and in process of arranging a trip back to London when my world crashed. My parents showed me a copy of the London Times with the announcement of the marriage of Francesca Brownlee to Vincent Barrington-MacNeil. Not two months had passed and she had already hooked up to another man. I felt betrayed.

'Later I discovered my parents had been working with hers to block our romance and I never forgave them.' Summerwest's eyes shone with a sudden radiance. 'But now, Jack, I've found her!'

Jack was moved. Even a stuffed shirt can have a heart.

'So what's with the locket and coin thing?' he asked.

'It's your passport into her presence. The important thing is that we can make contact again.' Summerwest opened his wallet and handed over a well-worn photograph.

'This is her all those years ago.'

'Quite a stunner,' Jack agreed, taking in the pretty, smiling face with its faraway look. 'But she was barely more than a kid.'

Summerwest passed over another picture.

'This is her today. I downloaded it from the internet.'

If time waits for no man, it had at least slowed down for Francesca Barrington-MacNeil. The dame in the photo could've easily passed for a sophisticated mid-thirty something, with the same cute smile to die for.

'On the internet?'

'As you know, I'm an aficionado of classical music and her son is getting to be a pretty famous musician. His professional name is Brendan MacNeil and I was checking out his website and there was a photo of him, and I thought, he has that same look as...and there was the name, of course. And then I noticed his date of birth. And I got so excited. It all fitted. I did further research and confirmed it. Francesca is his mother. It's fate, Jack, fate! That's why I came to England. To find out the truth. Was our love in vain? But I can't risk contacting her directly.'

Jack handed the photos back. So, he thought, he was being asked to play a part in reuniting a middle-aged Romeo with his Juliet who hadn't died after all. He posed the obvious objection.

'What about the Barrington-MacNeil guy?'

'It is, of course, vital he suspects nothing.'

'And all I have to do is take the locket to this dame and bring you her reply?'

'It's that simple. Her husband's a lawyer. He should be in court all day tomorrow.'

Jack knocked back another slug and pondered. That morning he had successfully carried out the task Mousy had sent him on and was feeling pretty good, so why not do the guy this favour?

'Okay, Carl,' he said, 'leave it with me. And make sure those tables are booked tight.'

The joy in Summerwest's eyes was palpable.

An attractive woman Jack recognised from the photo Summerwest had shown him opened the door of the penthouse apartment. She looked at him uncertainly and Jack couldn't help noticing the bruising around her left eye.

'Yes?' she said.

'I'm truly sorry to bother you, Mrs Barrington-MacNeil, but an old friend asked me to give you this.'

He held up the chain from which the locket hung and she tilted her head slightly as she gave it a puzzled look. After a few seconds one hand went to her mouth and her lips began to tremble. The other hand reached out and he lowered it into her open palm.

She fumbled to undo the clasp. The locket swung open and she took out the coin and peered at it. She gasped and put a hand to her rapidly paling face.

'Are you okay, lady?' Jack reached out to steady her.

'It's all right. I'm fine.'

'This comes with it.' He handed her Summerwest's letter.

She glanced down the hallway. 'Come in quickly.' Stepping back, she gestured him into the apartment, closed the door and preceded him swiftly down the hall into a sun-lit, richly-furnished sitting room with a scent of blossom and a magnificent view across the Thames. There was no sight or sound of any other occupant.

She perched on a high-backed chair, tore open the envelope and read the note. As she did so, Jack sat on the sofa and gave Francesca Barrington-MacNeil the once over.

Slim, wearing a plain, white blouse and black jeans, she reminded him of Barbara Stanwick in an old movie, the one where she plots with her lover to do away with her husband. But it was her face, still only faintly etched by time, which put her into a class of her own. It wasn't so much its beauty, being of the high-cheek-boned variety such as many actresses have, but its innocent-as-pie, little-girl helplessness that touched him. The sunlight made the bruising stand out more, but that barely diminished her attraction. No wonder Summerwest rejoiced at the chance to link up with her again. Hell, Jack thought, he was being drawn to her himself. He wondered if she had a thing for five-foot-two, sixteen stone gourmands.

She finished reading and looked up. Her eyes shone to match Summerwest's and the colour was back on her cheeks. She gazed across the room as though in a trance. She must have become aware of him staring at her, for she gave a start, ran a finger across her eye and said, 'You'd think I was old enough to know what doors can do when you walk into them.' She spoke with a self-deprecating laugh, rather unconvincing, Jack thought. Jack had heard tales like that from dames before and it had always meant the same thing. He felt angry, but said nothing.

'So you're Jack,' she continued, fluttering the note. She opened the locket again. 'The ambassador complete with insignia of office.'

She rose, placed the locket and note next to a vase and snapped off a newly opened rose. Stepping forward, she gently pushed it into his lapel, brushing off an invisible speck as she did so. Jack felt a surge of pleasure at the brief contact.

'Do you know Carl well?'

'Hardly at all,' he admitted. 'We met just three days ago in a hotel bar. I'm here on a business trip, met a fellow patriot and took it from there.'

'So, he's back in London,' she said dreamily. 'All those years I wanted to contact him, but didn't know how. At first I was a little desperate.' She shrugged. 'Time passes so quickly.'

'Mrs Barrington-MacNeil,' he said. 'Carl didn't explain nothin' about the coin. I know it's not my business, but I'm kinda curious.'

'Please', she said, 'call me Fran.'

He sat facing the window sipping coffee and staring at the locket she had placed in his palm, the twin of the one he had brought. Inside was a silver shilling, but with a man's head. Screwing up his eyes, he read the inscription: Georgius III Dei Gratia.

'His full name, Jack,' she explained, standing behind him with a light hand resting on his shoulder, 'is Carl George Summerwest III.'

'That figures,' he said. 'He talks like he has a pedigree and dresses like he's been entered for a show.' His brain kicked into action. 'George III? Well, I'll be damned! Do you have another name, Fran, that might just be Victoria?'

She moved round to the window seat, letting her fingers trail absently across his back. The touch was sensuous and no seduction was intended, Jack realised, but the thought was nice. What Carl must have gone through all those years, he couldn't imagine.

She sat and slipped one knee over the other. 'You've guessed. The coins were Carl's idea. He saw them in a shop window and we toured Hatton Gardens to find two lockets the right size that matched. They were to be our secret love tokens.' She smiled wistfully. 'We thought we had been touched by destiny.'

'I heard destiny took the day off.'

She gave a rueful grin. 'My parents disapproved, but they were tolerant of our relationship until Carl returned to America. Before Carl came along, they'd wanted me to marry Vince, the son of an old family friend, whom I had been seeing, and he waltzed back into my life the moment Carl left. It was all too easy for mum and dad to intercept Carl's letters and phone calls. They told me Carl had lost interest. In his eyes I was just a passing fling, they said, and told me to forget him. I accepted that all too easily and so I yielded to the growing pressure and married Vince. I should have been open with Vince from the beginning, but I was too spineless to admit how it had really been between Carl and me. Vince doesn't even know the true significance of the locket.'

Jack got the helpless look that so moved him.

'For thirty years I've longed to get in touch with Carl again.' She brushed a tear from her cheek. 'And now I can. Would you mind waiting while I pen a reply?'

His heart went out to her. Two lovers had been tricked out of love by meddling parents. It was time to put things right and he determined to do anything to help her get back with her old, true sweetheart.

Left by himself, Jack studied the photos that adorned a piano in a corner of the room. There was one of Fran (he could only think of her now as Fran) with a man he took to be Vincent Barrington-MacNeil. (He could never think of him as Vince.) There was also a gorgeous portrait of Fran and another in a matching frame, clearly from the same studio, of Barrington-MacNeil.

He looked carefully at the portrait of her husband. It wasn't flattering. There was a granite hardness about that square face with its flat nose, like a boxer's, and his thin, cold lips and indifferent, shark-like eyes. What if the louse wouldn't move over quietly? What if he used his bag of legal tricks to thwart his wife's reconciliation and deny her the settlement she deserved? Jack thought of the woman's bruising again. Some men didn't deserve dames.

There was also a photo of a younger man holding a violin. That must be the musician son Carl had mentioned. He picked it up for a closer look. Yes, there was that same smile. Thank God he took after his mother.

'That's my son Brendan.'

Fran was standing behind him. In her hand was an envelope.

'Carl told me he was a professional musician.'

'Yes. And a good one.'

She took the photo from him and replaced it before half turning towards the window and tossing her head to allow her long hair, golden in the late afternoon sun, to hang alluringly down. She looked fabulous.

A wall clock chimed.

'You'd better go,' she said. 'Vince phoned to say he would be home early today. Best if you don't meet.'

Jack sighed. It was time to stop cosying up.

She held out the envelope. 'Please give this to Carl.'

As they paused at the front door, she pressed the locket into his hand. The touch of her flesh was electric.

'Carl will be wanting this back.'

As he took it, she leaned forward and kissed his cheek. 'Thank you so much, Jack. I'm sure I don't have to ask you to be discreet.'

As the elevator carried him down, his brain bubbled over with possibilities. If Barrington-MacNeil became a problem, should he repay Summerwest's freebies with one of his own or offer him a deal at the going rate? Mousy wouldn't approve of moonlighting, but what Mousy didn't know wouldn't make him dyspeptic.

That evening, a cab took Jack and Summerwest to the Albert Hall. In the interval, they stayed in their box sipping a Brut Imperial that Summerwest got sent up from the Champagne Bar. Since Summerwest had read Fran's reply, he had blossomed into a light-hearted mood.

'Remember that London gangland killing on the news yesterday?' he chuckled. 'Can you believe it? The police now suspect the killer was outsourced from New York.'

Jack drained his glass and smiled. 'You don't say. They pick anybody up?'

'He'll be long gone. The mayor could hire him to clean up Manhattan South.'

'I doubt the city could afford it.' Jack held out his glass for a refill. 'You know, I didn't think this kinda music was me, but the Mozart stuff was pretty.'

'Then you should like Brahms' violin concerto.'

'Violin? Say, your lady-friend's son plays the violin.'

'I know,' Summerwest said. 'That's how I found her, remember?'

Jack lowered his voice. 'I guess one day you'll be meeting him when things have, er, worked out.'

'I've arranged for us to meet him after the concert,' Summerwest said with a superior smirk.

Jack's brain whirred again.

'Fran's son's the soloist!' he exclaimed. 'Of course! We're not here just to enjoy the music.'

'But, Jack,' Summerwest emphasised, 'he mustn't know. As far as he's concerned, we're just patrons of music.'

Jack raised his hands. 'Not from me! I guess he'll find out soon enough, anyways.'

Summerwest looked aghast. 'He must *never* know! I can't go around blundering into other people's lives. The damage it could do.'

'Er, Carl. How do you figure he won't know when you're together?'

'Together? With whom?'

'Fran.'

Summerwest looked puzzled. 'That's impossible, Jack. She has a husband. You know that.'

Jack felt exasperated. 'C'mon, Carl! Show some backbone! Y'can't leave that gorgeous gal with that brute.'

'Vincent Barrington-MacNeil is a brute?'

'He smacks her.'

'He what?'

'I seen the evidence. The black eye. She tried to cover it up. Some crap about a door. But I seen it too many times.'

'But he's a respected lawyer.'

37

'That's the worst sort! They know how to cover their tracks. Believe me, I got experience. And she also told me for thirty years she's been longing to get in touch with you again.' Jack leaned forward and mouthed, 'Carl, don't give up now. If the guy won't give way, I can arrange for him to be taken care of. And for a dame like Fran, you get my personal attention.'

'Taken care of?' Summerwest repeated. 'Is he unwell?'

'Don't act the dumb bunny, Carl! You know what I mean. Knock off, waste, zap. Or perhaps for your benefit I should've said given a one-way ticket to the hereafter!'

Summerwest's eyes almost exploded, his mouth opening and closing, until he finally blurted, 'You want to *kill* Vincent Barrington-MacNeil?' He put a hand to his mouth and looked round, but the adjacent boxes were empty. 'You're insane, Jack!' he hissed.

'I know you're a stuck up prig, Carl,' Jack retorted, 'but I never took you for a schmo. All those years wasted. And now you've been given the chance for some happiness you want to throw it away. For God's sake, Carl, follow your heart and save the woman you love.'

'The woman I love is in North Riverdale. My wife, Jack, is a very understanding woman, but she stops short at a ménage à trois preceded by murder! What on earth possesses you to imagine I want to run away with Francesca Barrington-MacNeil?'

'Don't be coy with me, Carl. I'm in too deep. The love tokens give you away. The coins that say, "Victoria loves George III and George III loves Victoria".'

'Jack, Jack, that was in another life. I've been happily married for twenty-five years, though Jennifer and I never had children.'

For a moment Summerwest continued to stare hard at Jack, then his eyes started to twinkle and his lips twisted into mirth. He clapped Jack squarely across the shoulders.

'Why, you old devil, Jack. You old joker. *I'm not going to ask you to kill someone*! I was a stuck up prig, wasn't I? But you paid me back in full. Pacino couldn't teach you a thing.'

'What about the black eye?'

'Even back then she was always walking into things.'

'Then I don't get it,' Jack said. 'What the hell's going on? What are you doing here? What's your angle with Fran?'

Summerwest beamed and fished in his inside jacket pocket.

'Have a cigar, Jack. Today I became a father!'

The Meeting Place

Meg Macleod

a room
two hundred years old
a window in the sloping roof
just big enough to hold the moon

reincarnated from exile
a night
beyond the grasp of memory

beginning slowly
toe to toe
thigh melding to thigh
intertwining arm to shoulder
the giving way of mouth to mouth

recognition

holding there as if in a storm
bodies knowing the pleasure
of belonging one to the other

Flow Country

Sharon Gunason Pottinger

Malcolm headed north. This time he was really in trouble. He had confided in his best friend – his only friend, Frankie. Frankie who stood by him all those times he was too drunk or too hot headed – he pounded the steering wheel with the heel of his hand – that damn temper of his. Frankie saw by the look on Malcolm's face that it was serious this time, so Malcolm went ahead and told him. Some pimps were mad at him for beating on their women. What the hell did they expect, after all? Real whores – not the everyday kind. He had yet to meet a woman that wasn't needing a lesson.

Not all women. Frankie's wife was the only honest woman in his life. When Malcolm had tried it on with her, she gave him a black eye, but she didn't tell Frankie. That was class. If they were all like her. But they weren't. Frankie, faithful Frankie, what was his advice? 'If you can't do 'em without beating on them, leave them alone fer Chrissakes.'

He drove through the night. The roads got smaller and the sky got darker. He drove until there was no more north. 'Thurso, northernmost town in Britain' the sign said. It was early morning. Only the bakery with a few tables in front was open. He got a full Scottish and watched the town wake up.

And he listened. He figured working people – his kind of people – would be coming in talking about the things he needed to know, like where to get a job. And that's how he happened to wind up as crew chief on the construction of an observation tower in the middle of a bloody bog on the far north of Scotland. He laughed to himself thinking how he'd spin the tale out for Frankie when he got back. It was just plain luck, but he'd make himself the hero of his story. And better yet. No bloody women up here to cause trouble for him.

He thought Thurso was the back of beyond, but when he got to the construction site, looking out over the so-called Flow Country there was really nothing here. They could jazz it up all they wanted for the punters. It was a whole lot of nothing, which suited him fine for now.

He didn't mind the controversy about not wanting a bloody great tower in the bog. Locals staying away made it possible for him to get the job. The 'No to the Tower' spray painted on the side of a barn on the way to the site didn't seem unusual to him. Graffiti of one kind or another was all part of his world.

The construction site, an observation tower being built by the bird-loving group, was perfect for him. There had been a bit of a panic when they discovered the body, but once they learned it was 200 years ago, only the archaeologists and a handful of reporters had been interested. Now only the hole remained – about the size of a grave – and rapidly filling with water. Things could disappear quickly up here. They had laid down a line of wooden pallets as a temporary walkway.

Times like this, after the crew had left, he was lord of all he could see. He had missed his century. He would have made a great war-lord. As he turned to pack up and leave, something in the parking lot caught his eye. A small red car with just one person in it. A bird lover or a walker he thought until she stepped out of the car. She wasn't dressed for walking. The skirt was too tight for anything but attracting attention. And she was wearing a jacket like a man's suit jacket. He hated when women did that. A bloody ball buster. What the hell was she doing out here on his site?

Williamina – Mina to her friends and in all her by-lines – had dressed with care for this interview, but it had been that long since she had worn her city clothes that they scarcely fit. Never mind, she told herself. This story about the local resentment of the community and the bird group would put her career back on track. She had emailed her former editor about a series of community vs quango articles and he had expressed some enthusiasm. Not as much as she had hoped, but enough to get her to pull the old clothes out of the closet and head out for a nosey.

Her trademark, when she had been a regular employee on the paper, was her hands on, balanced approach to any controversies. That's why her first stop was to see the site itself and talk to the people building it. What steps had they taken to ensure the damn thing wasn't going to sink into the bog? How had they persuaded planning to let them build an observation tower on a bog when so many other applications had been refused? But she'd save those questions for conversations with the big boys. Today, if she used her feminine wiles, she thought she might get a conducted tour of the construction in progress, maybe even a look at the plans and any stories about the things they'd found in the bog – like that body they found a couple of weeks ago.

As she walked the long gravelled path that wound around the wettest parts of the bog toward the tower, she stopped to glance at the signposts, 'sundew: the carnivorous plant', and 'sphagnum moss: once used for bandages for its ability to absorb moisture.' It will take more than that to get tourists up here, she thought. She had mixed feelings about tourism here – as did everyone. Visitors were welcome, of course, but somehow tourism seemed like a last resort. The fishing, the agriculture, forestry had faded. Sustainable energy had seemed like a great hope despite all the opposition. This same group that was building their tower on the peat had protested the last three wind farm applications – not safe to build on peat or peat needed to be protected or we needed to save the peat for the birds. And now here was their own tower built on the very peat they were pledged to be protecting. She shook her head to clear those thoughts. She needed to be able to be objective. None of the papers could or would send a reporter all the way up here. She was here and she had to make this story count. Neither she nor the place she loved deserved to be overlooked or turned into a piece of living history.

Malcolm watched her coming. He noted the way her skirt was higher in back than in front because her arse was so round and full. He stared at the horizon to calm himself, but the voices in his head were screaming, 'Another filthy whore. Coming here, she's asking for it.'

Even if Mina had read his expression or his body language, she was so eager for this new by-line and a chance to be a voice for local people, that she missed the danger signs.

Malcolm, warlord of his dominion, defender of purity, tried to rip her skirt away to teach her a lesson, but the buttons on her blouse gave way more easily. She struggled but Malcolm was an expert in combat with unsuspecting females and this one was no match for him.

'That'll teach her, the nosey besom,' he said when he realised there would be no more questions from her. He could say or do whatever he wanted. What he wanted to do right now was put this nosey reporter where no one would find her for another 100 or so years and he knew just how to do it.

The police and the archaeologists had already looked in that hole of theirs, so no one would look again. It was perfect. He didn't worry about dumping her and all her stuff into that hole and covering it over. If anyone asked, he'd say it was a hazard or that he wanted to ensure they kept to their schedule or some such, but who would ask? His crew wouldn't be back until morning and he often worked late.

He dragged her body off the edge of the tower toward the

hole where they had found that poor sod. Probably coming back from Culloden the archaeologists had said. Malcolm felt the strength surge in his arms. If he'd been with Braveheart, they would have won. In his stories to himself and to Frankie, he was always the hero. A dead woman in his arms was a detail that did not fit into his stories. He was able to overlook all the things that didn't fit his stories. But now he needed to move carefully stepping on the temporary walkway of pallets constructed to ensure no one got hurt. He laughed to himself, 'Safety first!' The pallets rocked a bit, and some seemed a bit lower than they had been, but it was an easy walk for him even dragging her dead weight. He rolled her body into the convenient hole along with her briefcase, laptop, mobile phone and handbag. Each one made a satisfying squish as it landed and quickly sank into the water-logged moss. 'If they find her in 100 years, they'll have a bloody great time capsule,' he laughed. He began shovelling nearby soil back into the hole – he didn't have to be tidy. Everyone knew there had been a hole here. No one would think anything of it.

The saturated soil was heavy. His shovel disappeared into a pool of red-brown liquid each time he inserted it, and the sticky liquid clung jealously to his shovel when he tried to lift it. He was sweating hard when he finished. His hands were covered with sticky red-brown streaks of wet peat which reminded him of blood. He hurriedly wiped his hands on his trousers. He'd clean up and get rid of these clothes – just in case.

He turned to make his way back to the tower and the walkway to the parking lot. The nearest pallet had begun to tip into the peat. 'Good,' he thought, 'saves us having to pick them up.' It was an easy step-hop onto the next pallet, but it teetered just below the surface, quickly soaking his boots and the cuffs of his trousers with cold, peaty brown water. 'Bloody hell!' The next pallet was already half submerged, but he thought he could stretch to the one beyond, which was riding high on one of the rare drier spots in this God-forsaken place. Why anyone would want to come here was beyond him. He missed the pallet.

Before he had time to collect his wits, he was up to his thighs in stale brown muck. Tourists might fall for all those stories about environmental this and that and history and such, but he knew muck when he saw it. He reached for the pallet he had so narrowly missed and began to pull himself up, but instead of rising, the pallet began to sink slowly beneath the surface. He scrambled like a drowning man struggling for air or earth or anything solid until his arms had no more strength and his lungs had lost their thirst for air.

The next morning his crew were baffled. 'His tools are here. Still on site. That's odd,' Willie said. 'And his car.'

'He must have stayed on site to fill in the hole the archaeologists made,' James said looking at the place where the last pallet still marked the site of the excavation. 'Were they finished? I thought they said they were coming back today.'

'Well, if so, we'll have to lay more pallets. The bog swallowed the ones we laid down.'

'Already? This place gives me the creeps.'

'What's the matter? Don't like ghosts?' Willie said, calling the boss's mobile number.

It took them a long cold moment to believe that the boss's ring tone was coming from under the peat. And less time to decide to leave without looking back.

Read more by Sharon

Something Slithered

Meg MacLeod

Something slithered at the edge of the pool of light from the porch, just beyond the focus of her eyes. She withdrew into the safe brightness of her kitchen. Fear stood behind her. She made the decision subconsciously. She would not go out. The idea blossomed slowly and irrationally, like a desert flower that became viable from a shower of rain. Her fear anointed the idea, gave it credence. She did not need to go outside, ever again. Doors were opened to let people in, windows, too, to let in the breeze.

Whatever slithered out there in the darkness trapped her. She was a willing prisoner, finding it restful and easy to reduce her life to simplicity. She ordered food from Tesco, her friend Martha moved the dustbins beside the window so she could do her duty and recycle, she told the council she could not go out and that they would have to collect them from the porch, thank you. There was no need to confuse herself with the outside. Her computer became the control room. She never missed the postie or the delivery men. Everything ran like clockwork. The garden got out of hand. She phoned for help. A very nice lady came to cut the grass and weed. Betty was not altogether perfect, being a bit careless, but she was reliable and the garden survived the slightly callous attention as if released from a too tight regime. She herself had been a meticulous gardener and felt a slight regret at giving it up. But her fear was too great. One day a nurse came to visit and enquired if she needed help.

'Of course not,' she said, made tea for the nurse and chatted about the politics of the moment. The news, on the hour, every hour, kept her well informed. The nurse noted the tidy garden, the Tesco shopping on the table. She failed to notice that which was hidden in the old ladies eyes. She ticked the box, 'Everything O.K.' and went away.

She would glance out sometimes towards the edge of the porch-light, straining her eyes to see into the shadowy corners. Of course, the slithering thing was just an excuse. She would have found another reason to avoid the outside, but knowing *it was there* justified her actions.

She prided herself on her ingenuity and organization. The car would be sold. Martha would do all the negotiating. They would be told to come during daylight hours so that they could get past the slithery thing; Martha would do the deal and that would be that. Perfect, but not quite. For all her planning she could not rearrange other people's worlds.

Late one night, there was a knock at the door. She peered through the safety lens. It was a young man. She opened the door a crack with the chain in place.

'I've come to see the car, heard it was for sale.' He spoke through the slit in the door. 'I'm off to the rig, need a car for the wife and bairn, urgent like. My gearbox went.'

'Come back tomorrow,' she replied, her eyes shifting beyond him to the darkening beyond the light.

'Can't, off at dawn to catch a flight, early train first thing.'

A deep sense of irritation knotted her stomach. She became thoughtful. 'How did you...?' her sentence remained unfinished, uncomfortable. He seemed familiar. She wondered how he had managed to get past the shadows. He shuffled in the silence that hung in the night between them

Her fear, always fluttering around her, began to rearrange itself becoming something much more threatening. He must go away. Her thoughts became disorganised. It was imperative to keep out the darkness. He must leave.

'Can't help you tonight,' she said abruptly and slammed the door. He had no right to be there. She could feel *it*. It had never been able to get so close. It was *his* fault.

She watched the man through the window prowling around the garage attempting a look at the car he so desperately needed. His shadow merged into the night and into her mind.

She was sitting with the phone dangling from her hand when the police and ambulance men came. The telephone operator had found it difficult to understand her. Obviously the lady was distressed. The conversation was disjointed. She said something about the slithering coming to the door and that she did want to sell the car but it was too late and that she thought he must have tripped because when she looked again he was lying against the rockery, very still. 'And I could not go out there because I never do,' she added.

A policeman handed her a cup of tea. Her fingers grasped it gratefully, fingers that left bloody prints all over the cup.

'Oh, what a mess,' she said,

The policeman took the cup and bagged it. 'I'll get you another one,' he said. He looked at his partner who shook his head. His eyes gestured to the bloody footprints that trailed from the door.

Out beyond the porch light something moved. Two men were carrying a stretcher out of her garden. She watched them anxiously, her eyes straining to see what else might be out there. Her bare feet were cold and like her hands, stained red.

Henpecked? Moi?

Jean McLennan

Well, yes, I'm not talking about the missus bending my ear. On retirement from city life eight years ago, Helen, the said missus, and I reflected on happy times of our respective childhoods when hens were part of our daily lives. We decided to recreate that part of the 'good old days'; Helen was looking forward to baking with our own fresh eggs and I was anticipating, with pleasure, consuming the fruits of her labours. We have never sold our surplus eggs; this was never to be a business, just an enjoyable hobby. As children we had had no responsibility for the family poultry, apart from occasionally feeding them, so little did we realise the steep learning curve we were about to embark upon.

Preparation was easy. We read up on the topic. Katie Thear's book, *Starting with Chickens* was useful. Following her advice, to protect our flock from the ravages of weather, foxes and provide them somewhere to roost, and hopefully lay, a henhouse was essential. I designed and built a substantial shed with all mod cons, ie perches. and nest boxes and added a conservatory at one end. A farmer neighbour, on receiving a reply to his questioning the purpose of the whole structure, commented, 'Good God. A hen hotel!'

The fun was about to begin. Our thirty Lomond Browns duly arrived, and totally lacking appreciation of their new five star billet and caring owners, they attacked us and our collie with as much ferocity as they could muster. We learned the hard way that new arrivals should be kept in the henhouse for a couple of days till they know and appreciate who supplies their food.

Speaking of food, their days are mainly spent scraping around, seeking out and consuming insects and worms, but that diet isn't adequate to keep them in healthy, egg-laying fettle. Mash, grain and greens are recommended supplements, but since our hens are pets, (most of them have names; all die of natural causes, mostly through old age – our ground is peppered with little graves – none has ever gone in the pot) we soon started experimenting with little treats that have become part of the daily ritual.

Breakfast consists of porridge and sultanas bought in bulk to the amusement of the supplier; bowing to convention, mash etcetera is the midday meal; and, at teatime they bicker over spaghetti with garlic. Picture one hen, having snatched up a long piece of pasta which is now hanging from her beak like an extra juicy worm, rushing away to where she is going to gobble it up with several others in hot pursuit accompanied by much squawking and flapping of feathers. For reasons only understood by a hen, that one long strand is far more appealing than the others still on the plate. In the evening each bird has a tiny ball of steak mince – nothing but the best. Our reading said apples are beneficial to hen health but when we offered the fruit, which we had painstakingly chopped up, ours gave it the cold shoulder. Determined to do our best for our feathered friends, we added apple to their morning porridge. Later that day every hen was either staggering about or lolling in a dust scrape, drunk; the apple had fermented in their crops.

There is a pecking order and one does rule the roost. This is the derivation of those two expressions. Daisy, the boss, controls when all retire to the henhouse for the night and woe betide any who should attempt to enter before her. She will peck the audacious usurper mercilessly. Collectively the flock picks its enemies wisely. A foolish crow landed on the henhouse one day, and as one, they went into attack mode stripping the crow of its feathers and killing it. However, when a buzzard came to call not one hen was to be seen; they were all hiding under our caravan.

One of our neighbours owns a caravan site and he tipped us off that his cat, who was terrified of the hens was losing its breakfast every morning to one of them. Next day we positioned ourselves to watch. The miscreant jumped onto a wall, looked around stealthily, as if checking whether she was being observed, dropped down to the other side, and hurried round to the neighbour's porch where she scoffed the cat's breakfast. The cat wasn't her only victim. On another morning one of the caravaners left his bacon and egg on his table to answer a call of nature leaving his door open. He returned to an empty plate and contented hen roosting on the table. We find a regular supply of fresh eggs keeps us on good terms with our neighbour.

Having worked in the city we are regularly visited by townie friends and former work colleagues. One of them was hen-hating and thought the flock were deliberately intimidating her. They pursued her to her car when she went for a smoke. They lined up, perched on the adjacent fence staring at her when she was in the car, and after her cigarette they chased her back into the house. Unsurprisingly, she had no stomach for joining us outside for a seat in the sun where often a hen would perch on one of our shoulders parrot-like.

Early on in our henkeeping experience we decided one of our hens was unwell and needed attention from the vet. We knew this would be unusual but we take our hens' health and welfare very much to heart. A hen costs about £5, so no-one in their right mind who was in it for the money would welcome a vet's bill. In the vets' crowded waiting room a small dog approached my cat basket with its precious cargo and sniffed.

'He'll not harm your cat,' said the elderly owner.

'It's not a cat,' I replied.

'What kind of dog is it?' another woman asked.

'It's not a dog,' I replied. There was a long silence, the atmosphere becoming more tense by the second. The small dog was kept firmly reeled in beside its owner, perhaps they thought I had a dangerous animal.

'What is it then?' a little girl blurted out.

I answered quietly, but not quietly enough. An elderly farmer leaning on the counter laughed.

'An old hen!' he squawked. 'I never heard the likes. We would normally pull their necks.'

The vet was bemused when confronted with our off-colour bird. Poultry vet science is esoteric and usually exclusively practised on show birds. However a tonic was prescribed and the patient survived. Nowadays if one of the flock is unwell she is taken into our warm living room, in a cat basket, for a couple of nights. We think that some have become Emmerdale fans and may now be faking indisposition to keep up with their favourite soap.

Early on, the henhouse a mirror installed just inside the entrance and old CDs hanging from the roof beside the perches to provide a distraction; they peck at these instead of each other. First thing in the morning when the door is opened and they file out each hen appears to check her appearance in the mirror as she passes.

Our hens cluck and peck about in their run all day except when the veg plot has been cleared when they can roam over the whole smallholding. Preparing the ground for planting veg can be in turn amusing and frustrating as they get in about every spadeful looking for worms. For the more adventurous among them there's always the caravan site and neighbours' gardens.

We like to think our hens are happy as far as poultry are capable of experiencing that emotion. When they wriggle on their backs, legs in the air, enjoying a dust bath, it's hard to believe they are not in ecstasy and they provide us with a lot of pleasure and entertainment as well as a regular supply of eggs.

Recently Helen found a knitting pattern for a hen jacket and now she's located a particular yarn that reflects light. So, if you should spot a hen in a hi-vis jacket you've likely found us. Do pop in for a cup of tea and a piece of home baked cake, or even, if you are lucky, an omelette.

The Wizard of Caithness

John Knowles

Rain lashed the windscreen as Graham and Julia Bazalgette pulled onto the driveway of their new-build home near the Caithness village of Dunnet. A sudden flash zigzagged across the leaden sky and a second later an almighty crash shook the ground. The storm was right overhead and growing in intensity. Graham switched off the ignition and looked at Julia. He knew she'd had reservations about moving to Caithness. It was far away from friends and family, but the decision to relocate to the far north of Scotland had been a joint one. The couple, in their early forties, didn't have children, which made the decision easier.

Graham had secured a position with a computer software company in Thurso, and Julia a part-time receptionist at the local doctor's surgery.

'Have you got the key?' asked Graham.

Julia fumbled in her purse and brought out a shiny new key, which she handed to her husband. Another flash and crack of thunder ripped across the murky sky. Graham pushed hard against the howling gale as he opened the driver's door. After stepping onto a nearly-flooded driveway, he made a dash for the house. Fumbling with the key he slotted it into the lock and gave the door a shove. It flew open and he fell into the hallway.

Julia followed and soon they were both inside, wet and bedraggled.

The removal van wasn't arriving until the following day, so they slept on an airbed. Graham dropped off as soon as his head hit the rolled up trousers that doubled as a pillow. Julia had a restless night, kept awake by the wind as it whistled relentlessly around the house. All through the night, she was aware of an intermittent tapping on the bedroom window. Her imagination ran wild. Was there someone tapping on the glass or was it just branches blowing against the window?

The following morning she woke to bright sunshine streaming through the window. The wind was still howling, but at least the rain had stopped. Graham slept on. Julia slipped into her dressing gown and tiptoed downstairs to put the kettle on. As it came to the boil, she heard a thud against the front door.

She opened the door, expecting to see the removal van. There was nobody there. Then to her horror, she noticed a large dead crow lying on the doormat. She stared at it, transfixed. It must have flown into the door and been stunned, she thought. The unfortunate bird was buried in the garden later that morning.

They'd been in the house a couple of weeks and were settling in. The last of the boxes had been unpacked and the house was beginning to feel like home. The garden, however, looked like a bombsite. The design was a job for Graham and his computer. Julia couldn't wait to get started.

'Buddleia, we've simply got to have a Buddleia,' Julia said, as they sat drinking their morning coffee. She flicked enthusiastically through the pages of her Gardeners' World.

'Um, if you like, darling,' Graham muttered, engrossed in his computer magazine.

'Graham, you haven't heard a word I've said have you?'

'Sorry, darling, what was that?'

'Oh never mind, I can see you're more interested in boring computers than helping me plan the garden.'

Julia picked up a pen and started to make a list of the plants and bushes she wanted. Within ten minutes she'd drawn up a list as long as the A9.

'Right, put that magazine down, Graham. We're going to the garden centre to see if they've any of these plants.' She waved the list under his nose. She wasn't going to take no for an answer. As she walked into the hall, she thought she saw the fleeting shadow of a figure disappearing up the stairs. When she looked again it had gone.

She ran upstairs, looking inside each room in turn. They were all empty. When she came downstairs, Graham was standing in the hall looking bemused.

'What's the matter, darling?' he said, zipping up his jacket.

'I thought I saw someone going upstairs.'

'It was probably just a trick of the light. Come, darling, you said you wanted to go to the garden centre.'

The next morning Julia was up early. Pondering over the figure she thought she'd seen on the stairs, she'd had a restless night. Wandering half asleep into the bathroom, she switched on the light. A man with long white hair and a beard stared back at her from the mirror. She screamed. Within the blink of an eye, the face had gone. Her hands trembled as, trying to make sense of what she'd seen, she stared at her own reflection. Maybe she'd imagine this as well. Perhaps she was going insane.

Graham came rushing into the bathroom. 'What on earth's the matter, darling, you look like you've seen a ghost!'

Julia burst into tears and collapsed into his arms. 'I saw a man's face in the mirror, an old man with long white hair and a beard.'

'Are you sure? Maybe it was just a remnant of the dream you had last night. Come on, darling, I'll make you a nice cup of tea.'

With no more sightings, life fell into the familiar pattern of work, household chores and landscaping. By late May, the weather had begun to warm up. The lighter evenings enabled Julia to work outdoors until well after nine. They'd decided to employ a professional gardener to lay the lawn, but the borders were Julia's territory.

It was just before seven and Julia was digging at the bottom of the garden, when her spade struck something solid. After carefully scraping the soil away, she found a flat object about twelve inches wide and about two feet long.

Graham sat in his study working on his new computer.

Julia rushed in, hands encrusted with soil. 'Graham, I've found something strange in the garden. You've got to come and look.'

Graham sighed. 'I'm busy, darling. Can't it wait until morning?'

'No Graham, you've got to come now.' She led him through the house and down the path.

As he approached the border, Graham looked in surprise at the metallic stick embedded in the ground. He dug carefully around it with a trowel, and pulled the object out of the earth. In his hand it felt smooth, but icy cold too. Made of bronze, it had a small skull at one end and a shaft that tapered down to a point at the other. They stared at it in silence.

'I'll take it inside and give it a wash,' Graham said, frowning.

Once under the cold tap, the remaining soil fell away, revealing an ornately patterned shaft, the skull ugly and menacing.

'I'm not sure I want that thing in the house, Graham, it's hideous,' said Julia.

Graham laughed, ruffling her hair.

'Oh come on, darling. I'm sure it's perfectly harmless. You never know, it may be really old and worth something. Tell you what, I'll see if I can track down an antique dealer or someone with local history knowledge and see what they make of it.'

'Oh for God's sake, Graham, shove it in the cupboard under the sink for now. We'll decide what to do with it tomorrow.'

Graham opened the cupboard door and placed it inside a plastic bucket. 'Come on, darling, I'll give you a hand with the garden.'

The following day Julia had already left when Graham emerged from the bathroom. Having the day off work he decided to research the peculiar object they'd found. An Internet search proved fruitless. Then he recalled a recent visit to Castletown Heritage Centre. There'd been plenty of local history on display there. Marching into the utility room, he flung open the cupboard door and reached in, fumbling for the peculiar artefact. Bringing it into the light, to his surprise, he noticed that the small bronze skull had turned black.

Nothing oxidizes that quickly, he thought, and besides, bronze oxide would be green. Quickly he wrapped it in an old towel and shoved it into his rucksack.

A short man, about seventy years old with longish grey hair, was sitting in the main exhibition room of the Heritage Centre reading a book. He stood up and smiled as Graham entered. On his previous visit he had been greeted by a woman.

'Good morning sir, welcome to Castletown Heritage Centre. Are you up here on holiday?'

'Oh, no, I live here. Well, my wife and I moved to Dunnet a couple of weeks ago, so we're still finding our feet. I was hoping you might be able to help me with a little local history.'

'I'll do my best, sir.'

Graham pulled the object from his rucksack and unwrapped it. 'My wife found this in the garden and we were wondering what it was.' He held it out to the man, who suddenly became quite agitated.

'Oh no sir, I don't need to handle it. I'm afraid I've no idea what it is. Where is it you live, if you don't mind me asking?'

'We're in the new house overlooking Black Loch on Dunnet Head.'

The man backed off slightly, staring at the object as if transfixed by it. 'There is someone, Morag Sutherland. She lives at Windy Nook Cottage in Gunn's Lane, here in Castletown. What she doesn't know about this area isn't worth knowing. She's getting on a bit and is a little deaf, but I'm sure she'll help.'

Wrapping the bronze curio in the towel, Graham put it back in his rucksack, thanked the curator and left.

It didn't take long for Graham to find Windy Nook Cottage. The single storey building had whitewashed walls with a sky blue door and window frames. Remembering the woman's deafness, Graham banged on the door. A short, slight woman with white hair appeared. Her vivid blue eyes looked at him enquiringly.

'Why didn't you ring the bell, young man?' She pointed to a small bell push attached to the doorframe.

'Oh, I'm sorry, I didn't see it,' Graham replied, somewhat embarrassed.

'I don't know, you young people can't see beyond the end of your nose. Now what can I do for you, young man? You're not a salesman are you?'

Graham laughed. 'Oh no, I'm not a salesman. Actually I'm after a little help regarding local history. The gentleman at Castletown Heritage Centre told me to speak to Morag Sutherland at Windy Nook.'

With that she gestured that he come inside. 'I'm Morag, and you?'

'The name's Graham, Graham Bazalgette.'

Well Graham Bazalgette, please come inside and I'll put the kettle on. Then you can tell me exactly how I can help.'

The old woman showed him into the front room. The furniture was from the 1960's and had seen better days. Parts of the carpet were threadbare. Books stood in crooked piles. She pointed to an old leather armchair. 'You sit down and I'll make some tea.'

Before long he heard the rattle of cups. Pushing open the door with her foot, Morag tottered in carrying a tray with tea and digestive biscuits. 'There we are, dear, help yourself to milk and sugar and do have a biscuit. Now what can I do to help, young man?'

Taking a deep breath, Graham told her about how he'd recently moved up to Caithness from London.

The old lady listened intently as she sipped her tea.

'So where in Dunnet did you build your house?'

Graham told her, and added, 'It's such a beautiful spot, very isolated and quiet, just what we wanted. Well it was until my wife decided that we had a ghost.'

'A ghost you say?'

Graham smiled. 'I know, I've told her not to be so ridiculous.'

A worried look flashed across Morag's face.

'Is anything the matter, Mrs Sutherland?' he asked.

'So the legend is true,' she said.

'What legend?'

'The legend of Lachlan Fergus MacGregor, known by some as the Caithness Wizard. Lachlan lived over four hundred years ago. He's said to have inhabited a cave not far from here at Peedie Sands. Legend says he was murdered by locals for practicing witchcraft. Others believe he was innocent and simply a healer who made potions for the sick. The legend goes that his severed head was tossed over Holborn Head near to Thurso and his body buried at Dunnet overlooking the Black Loch.'

Graham drained his teacup, and leaned forward, eager to find out more about Lachlan Fergus MacGregor.

'It is said that Lachlan will never rest in peace until his innocence is recognised and he's avenged.' Morag smiled and reached for the plate of biscuits. 'Have another biscuit. Now what was it you wanted advice about?'

Pulling the bronze object from his rucksack Graham held it up to show her.

Fear radiated from her eyes as she stared at it. She pulled herself up from the chair and shuffled over to where Graham was sitting. Eventually she spoke. 'May I look?' Taking it from him, she ran her hand over its ornately engraved shaft.

'I've seen a drawing of something similar to this in a book about Highland myths and legends. I'm pretty certain that what you have here is Lachlan's magic wand.'

'A magic wand, oh come on, you're kidding! Surely you don't expect me to believe it's a magic wand?'

'If I were you, I'd throw it in the sea and forget about it.' Her expression sent a shiver down Graham's spine.

He frowned. 'Oh no, I couldn't do that. If it's as old as you are suggesting it could be worth a lot of money.'

She handed it back to him. 'Whatever it's worth, it'll bring you nothing but bad luck. If you've built your house over Lachlan's grave, you'll never be at peace there.'

Graham drove away from Windy Nook pondering what Morag had said. He was naturally sceptical and viewed Morag's tale as a fanciful local myth with no substance in reality.

Later that night he and Julia sat in the living room watching television when suddenly Julia jumped up. 'Graham, can you hear that?'

Graham looked up from his 'PC Expert' magazine. 'I can't hear anything, darling.'

'It sounds like water pipes banging.'

'No, can't hear a thing.' He went back to his magazine.

As Julia crept upstairs the noise became louder. It seemed to emanate from the airing cupboard. She pulled open the door and looked inside. The pipes to the hot water tank were definitively resonating. Suddenly the noise stopped and the house was deathly silent. She felt something touch her head and froze, unable to breath. It felt like icy fingers had stroked her hair. Turning around slowly she saw a dark shadow disappear down the stairs.

Her scream brought Graham racing to her side. He enveloped her in his arms.

'Darling, whatever is it?' She was shaking uncontrollably, tears rolling down her cheeks.

'I can't live here Graham. There's something strange going on in this house. Someone touched my hair, I felt it! We've got a ghost.'

'I doubt it, darling. I thought they hung around old houses, not new ones.' As far as he was concerned, everything had a logical explanation.

'Are you sure you didn't imagine it, darling?'

She pulled away from him, a look of indignation on her face. 'No, I didn't imagine it, Graham. I'm telling you, someone or something touched my hair and then disappeared down the stairs.'

Graham sighed. 'Well nobody passed me on my way up.'

She detected a touch of impatience in his voice.

'Tell you what, if it'll makes you feel better, I'll have a word with the local minister and see what he suggests.'

Reverend Angus MacDonald was a tall, slight man with bright ginger hair. The reverend listened intently as Graham told him what his wife claimed to have seen.

'It all seems to have started when she found this in the garden.' Graham pulled the wand-like object out of a plastic bag and presented it to minister, who examined it carefully.

'I can't say I've seen anything quite like this before. These patterns look almost pagan. I'm afraid Ghost busting is beyond my remit. Have a word with Morag Sutherland. She's very knowledgeable when it comes to local history.'

Graham smiled. 'Oh I've already been to see her. For some strange reason, she seemed rather scared of it. She told me to throw it into the sea.'

The reverend handed it back to him. 'Morag scared? Granted it isn't exactly attractive, but it's not like her to be frightened. Maybe you should get rid of it, although I couldn't condone throwing it into the sea. Perhaps you should ask a Catholic Priest to perform an exorcism at your house. Alternatively I understand there's a Pagan Federation, but as a representative of the church, I'm reluctant to encourage them.'

Driving home Graham decided to take the minister's advice and just get rid of the wand. He was, however, reluctant to involve the church or a load of pagans. Then it came to him. He'd sell it on eBay and make a little money. Surely some new-age hippy would see it and be unable to resist such an unusual object. Within a week he'd received a bid of £40 from someone in Glastonbury. Accepting the bid, he duly parcelled the wand up and posted it to its new owner. It came as quite a surprise when a week later Graham received a rather terse e-mail from the buyer, wanting to know where his purchase was. He rattled off a reply, explaining that it had been dispatched. A further week passed and he was arranging a refund for the disappointed customer.

The coffee mug flew past Graham's left ear smashing on the kitchen wall behind him. The mug's remnants dribbled down the wall, pooling on the tiled floor below.

'How dare you suggest I'm making it up? I'm telling you, this house is haunted. I want to go back to London.' Julia's face was red with anger.

Graham stood there, still stunned by the violent outburst. In all the years they'd been together, she'd never lost her temper so completely.

'Well, how come I've never seen this supposed ghost?' he said, fighting the anger welling up inside.

'I don't know why,' she replied abruptly. With that she burst into tears and ran out into the hall.

He followed trying to put a comforting arm around her shoulder.

She pulled away. 'I'm scared Graham. Can't you see? We should sell this God-forsaken place and go back to London.'

Sighing, he put on his coat and picked up the car keys. 'I think its best if I go out for a while and give you time to cool off.'

The Northern Sands Hotel was busy with tourists mainly from the caravan park beside the beach. The aroma of home cooking wafted from the kitchen as a petite young waitress carried out some meals. He bought an alcohol-free beer and sat down in the corner. He hated it when he and Julia rowed, but moving back to London was the last thing he wanted. He nursed his pint for almost an hour, before leaving and going for a long walk on Dunnet beach. Dusk was descending as he climbed back into his Range Rover. In the distance he could see a plume of smoke rising up into the still evening air. And then he saw the familiar blue flashing lights of a fire engine.

Another heather burning fire that's got out of hand, he thought as he continued up the road towards the house.

As he turned the corner, to his horror, he realised the smoke was coming from his house. It was on fire. He swung the motor into the drive and leapt out, leaving the engine running. Two fire engines sat in the driveway, with fire fighters training a jet of water onto the house. The lead fire fighter turned as Graham sprinted up to the fire tenders.

'I'm Graham Bazalgette, owner of this property. My wife's in there.' Looking up at the burning building, Graham saw Julia at the bedroom window. 'Julia, Julia,' he screamed, rushing forward.

One of the fire fighters seized his arm and held him back. 'No, you can't go inside sir. It's not safe.'

Suddenly, in the window, a dark figure appeared behind Julia but disappeared in an instant.

'Thank God one of your men managed to get up to her.'

Leading fire fighter Alec Gow gave Graham a puzzled look. 'I'm sorry sir; but none of my men have entered the house yet. The fire's too intense to affect an entry at ground level, so we're going to put a ladder up to the first floor.'

'But I saw someone else at the bedroom window with her. There's definitely somebody in there.' His hand shook, as he pointed to the window. There was no one there.

'Like I said sir, there are no fire fighters in the building as yet.'

Alec Gow, barked instructions to his men to extend the ladder to the first floor. As they did so, Julia's face reappeared at the window, but this time she was alone. As one of the fire fighters scaled the ladder, an ambulance skidded to a halt, and two paramedics leapt out. Within minutes Julia was being loaded into the ambulance and inside the hour she was lying in a hospital bed in Wick, undergoing treatment for smoke inhalation. She'd been lucky and hadn't suffered any burns. Two days later, she was discharged from hospital. Graham had managed to arrange rental accommodation through the insurance company.

The temptation to visit their house ate away at Graham. He wanted to see the damage for himself. He'd already questioned Julia as to how the fire had started, but she'd no idea. She'd just smelt smoke and called the fire brigade. She'd tried to escape, but the fire had trapped her upstairs.

'Don't you think we should see what's left of the house, darling?'

She shook her head. 'No Graham! I don't want to see that house again. I nearly died in there remember. There's something evil there. You go if you really want to.'

He placed a kiss on her forehead. 'Okay, if that's what you want. I only want to take a few photographs for the insurance company. I know they'll send someone up, but I'd rather take a few myself, just to be on the safe side.'

A fire service car was parked on the drive when Graham arrived. The sheer devastation shocked him. The place had been raised to the ground. A couple of fire fighters were going through the ruins. One of them recognised him and raised a hand.

'So, any clues as to how the fire started?' Graham said.

'Not yet, but we found something rather unusual. We didn't quite know what to make of it.' Delving into the boot of his car, the fireman pulled out a clear plastic bag and handed it to Graham.

Graham's heart thudded in his chest; a feeling of panic overwhelmed him. He examined the object with unbelieving eyes. 'Where did you find this?' he stammered, staring at the wand and into the eye sockets of the blackened skull.

'It was sticking out of the garden, over there.' The fireman pointed to the flower bed where Julia had first found it.

'But that's impossible; I sold it on eBay weeks ago. I don't understand how it's ended up back here.'

The fireman shrugged. 'Well you do what you like with it. It's not going to help us with our investigations.'

While driving back to Thurso, Graham decided his only option was to contact Morag Sutherland. He was convinced she knew more about the wand than she was letting on. All he wanted now was to rid himself of it and the bad luck it attracted.

Morag didn't seem surprised when he called on her the following day. She listened as he told her about his house burning down and that the wand had been found in the garden.

She thought for a moment as she sipped on her tea. 'The way I see it, there is only one course of action. The ghost of Lachlan MacGregor has to be put to rest once and for all.' She gave him an almost apologetic smile. 'You may find this hard to believe, but I am in fact a high priestess of the pagan religion. I have pagan friends who can deal with a haunting of this kind. I could conduct a special ceremony that will drive the spirit of Lachlan from these lands forever, but I'll need your cooperation.'

Graham frowned. 'Oh, I'm not sure I want to get involved in any black magic or strange stuff like that.'

'But you will have to. I cannot remove the curse, without your complete cooperation. After all, you chose to build a house over Lachlan's grave.'

Graham thought about her proposal. What had he got to lose? He didn't think for one minute that the old woman had any extraordinary powers. Another voice in his head warned him not to get involved, but he waved it away.

'Okay, but as long as my wife is not told about this. She's suffered enough.

Morag put her tea cup down. 'Oh no, it's just you we need there. Meet me on Holborn Head next Wednesday evening at nine o'clock. We will be waiting for you beside the cairn. Don't forget to bring Lachlan's wand. It's vitally important that the wand is present at the ceremony.

Wednesday evening soon came around. Graham told Julia he'd some work to do that he couldn't get out of.

Driving along Thurso seafront towards Scrabster, he could see Holborn Head and the lighthouse in the distance. Darkness was beginning to fall as he climbed the narrow path. He reached the brow of the hill. In the distance he could see a group of people standing in a circle, each wearing a purple hooded cloak.

As he approached, they turned to face him, before lowering their hoods. To his astonishment he recognised both curators from Castletown Heritage Centre as well as two of the firemen that had attended his burning house. One of the firemen held a flaming torch. Morag strolled across and greeted him.

'Have you brought the wand?'

He took it out of his rucksack and handed it to her.

The sun was just disappearing below the horizon, turning the sky a delicate fusion of orange, pink and red.

She gestured that he enter the circle of ten men and ten women. Standing beside him and facing the north, Morag raised her arms to the heavens. Then in a voice that belied her petite stature, she started to speak.

'Before me stands Thor.
Behind me Vali.
At my right hand Mani.

At my left hand Loki.
Before me flames the pentagram.
And above me the six-rayed star.

Oh mighty wizard, Wizard of Caithness,
accept this mortal as a sacrifice.
We pray that this will appease you.'

Graham, looked in disbelief at the solemn faces of the pagan worshippers who encircled him.

'Wizard? Sacrifice? What do you mean? I thought we were here to banish the ghost of Lachlan MacGregor.'

A stocky, brutish man broke from the circle, joining Morag and Graham at its centre. His strong, muscular arms grabbed hold of Graham's and held him in check. Graham fought to break free, but the man was too strong.

'Let me go,' he screamed, continuing to resist.

Morag turned to face him and spoke serenely. 'Those who desecrate the grave of the Wizard must pay. Proceed with the ceremony.'

In unison the pagans burst into song. Hand in hand they danced around him. It was a melodic tune about the earth, sky and sea. Without warning the circle broke and the singing stopped. Graham was being pushed closer to the cliff edge. All that could be heard now was the sea crashing on the rocks below and the squawk of seagulls. Three sharp chants and Graham Bazalgette disappeared over the edge.

The Chemistry Boys

Irena Bracey

The Police would have a job finding any evidence, but the motive was clear to Phyllis. How long would it be before they came knocking on their door and the lies would start again?

Remembering that day when her boys came home gave Phyllis a dreadful feeling in the pit of her stomach. She decided to sleep on it before she mentioned her dark thoughts to her husband.

The summer holidays had begun, holidays that would have no end for Ben and Jack because they were not going back to finish their degrees. Not after the results of the tribunal where they were accused and found guilty of plagiarism.

Professor Lowe was the main accuser and his evidence had swung things the wrong way for them. A few other misdemeanours were thrown in for good measure and the result was that they were sent down for good.

After they overheard the professor telling other students how he intended to spend the first day of his vacation, something about taking a nostalgic trip, the two brothers decided to take a train journey. They thought this was perfect, just the ticket since they were at a loose end and dreading going back home to face their parents' disapproval.

When they got to the station, the train was ready for its excited passengers. The two young men were as keen to get on board and start the journey as the others. They were happy to share a carriage, and their fellow traveller was already seated by the window. They greeted the older man who nodded in return.

'You like trains, too?' he asked, surprise in his voice as they obviously didn't strike him as the average train spotters.

'Indeed we do.'

This was no ordinary train. Volunteers had restored the four vintage carriages to the way they used to look in the 50/60s. Long corridors with compartments off them, windows that opened, the old check upholstery and steel luggage racks. Even Ben and Jack could appreciate the good work which had gone into the refurbishment. It reminded them of the old films their parents liked to watch. They tried making conversation with the man, but it was obvious he would rather watch the scenery outside than chat to them, so they left him alone and talked to each other.

He was wearing the obligatory uniform of the train buff, a brown anorak and faded brown corduroy trousers, and carrying a small book, full of timetables, they assumed, something railway-related anyway. When he wasn't looking out of the window, he was glancing at it. Occasionally he would take a pencil out of his top pocket and make a note, put the pencil away and continue staring out of the window. Sometimes he would glance over at them, but turned his head away quickly if they noticed.

Their mother Phyllis couldn't have children and sadly came to the conclusion that motherhood wasn't meant for her. Then a friend introduced her to a young woman who had been a surrogate. The idea was sown and that was how she managed to have her children. Twins. Two lovely boys, more than she had hoped for. She and Frank were delighted.

Ben and Jack had been close from the start, almost inseparable. Phyllis found them a handful from the minute she took them home, but loved being a mum and presumed all parents of twins had the same problems.

They fought a lot as young boys do and she never could get the truth out of them as they closed ranks when any sign of discipline came their way. Frank helped as much as he could, but the job he had to take after his redundancy meant he had a longer commute so, by the time he got home, Phyllis had administered any punishment as best she could. For her, "Wait till your Father comes home" was not an option.

They were bright, intelligent boys, but naughty and as they got older became more and more mischievous and trouble was always round the corner. Phyllis was forever apologising for their tricks and delinquent behaviour.

Soon she was being called in by the headmaster more and more frequently as their pranks and general behaviour deteriorated. Bullying was mentioned, lying, cheating, fighting, verbal and physical abuse. They were often temporarily suspended, but this punishment did not deter them in their quest for disruption. Eventually Phyllis felt she needed therapy more than they did.

They were bored, so the chemistry lessons came as a God-send and just in the nick of time. They both liked their new teacher and loved the subject. The experiments held a fascination for them with all sorts of planned and unplanned explosions inside and outside the confines of the chemistry lab. They loved learning the symbols and formulas and the smells of the bubbling liquids in the test tubes.

They were hooked. Their passion led to good exam results enabling them to apply for universities. To everyone's surprise they managed to get into the same one. Their neighbours breathed a sigh of relief when term started, and they all came to wave off the over-packed car when Frank drove them away.

As the carriages rattled along, the ex-students tried to talk to their travelling companion once more, but he avoided eye contact and responded by nodding or shaking his head. The ticket collector came round in the full uniform of the day and punched their tickets. He told them that the buffet car was open.

'Do you take sugar in your coffee?' Ben asked the man who shook his head in reply and made a movement to get up to get his own.

'No, no, you sit there. Let me get these.' He gestured to Jack to stay with the older man while he went for the drinks. When he came back, they starting talking to each other, but in a stage whisper this time. They didn't care if the old man heard them.

'If it wasn't for *that* man we could have had that research on toxicology published and Mum would have been so proud of us for once. *He* said we'd breached academic integrity just because we *forgot* about adding the references. *He's* ruined it all for us now.'

They were hoping the older man would be provoked into saying something, anything, to give his opinion or thoughts on their predicament. But no, it seemed he found it hard to say anything at all.

The tribunal had been awful and Phyllis had cried with shame. 'How could they even think of taking someone else's hard work and pass it off as their own? I thought they were smarter than that. I am so disappointed,' she said. She wasn't going to listen to any of their excuses.

It was an act of fraud and she understood why they had to be expelled. She'd asked Frank where their parenting skills had gone wrong and even blamed the surrogate mother of passing on bad genes.

While Phyllis and Frank waited for the twins to come home to see what they had to say for themselves, Ben and Jack exited the train. There was one more station to go before the train made its way back, but they thought it was time to leave the past and return to the present. They hitched a lift home and were full of praise for their dip into history, tales of which they thought their parents would enjoy.

Phyllis did not share their enthusiasm for the railways and was saddened, but not surprised, to see they showed no signs of remorse for their disgraceful actions in university.

The next morning Frank left the paper open on the kitchen table, but it was his wife who noticed the article.

PROFESSOR RICHARD LOWE FOUND DEAD

Professor Richard Lowe was found dead on a vintage train on the first day of the university holidays. Two young men, who are believed to have shared his carriage, are being sought as witnesses so they can be eliminated from the enquiries.

The public are advised to contact the incident room with any information on 0123-456789.

Phyllis had a dreadful feeling in the pit of her stomach. She caught up with her husband by the front door.

'Frank I'm frightened. Do you remember how they were yesterday when they came home?'

'We'll talk about it when I get home tonight.'

The following day the paper had a few more details. It appeared that the Professor had been poisoned, probably cyanide, and the Police were treating his death as murder. Witnesses were being sought and an urgent appeal had been made to find the two young men who had shared a carriage with the dead man and may have been the last ones to see him alive.

Frank and Phyllis talked until the early hours.

All cried out, Phyllis couldn't take anymore. 'The police will have a job finding any evidence, I bet they made sure of that. Everyone will soon know they had a motive though. What are we going to do?'

Frank didn't answer. They'd said it all. They knew they had no choice. With his arm around her shoulders and with her heart breaking, Phyllis picked up the phone.

The Montpelier

Margaret Mackay

A grey afternoon in March; grey was the colour that came to mind on this sad occasion. It was the colour of the lowering bank of clouds casting dark shadows on the dry-stone dykes bordering the village kirkyard that sloped to the shores of the North Sea. Today, the sea had also donned its silver-tipped mantle. Grey was the colour of sorrow. Sorrow that seeped like sea mist into the hearts and minds of those present.

A persistent drizzle marred the surface of the inscribed brass plate: Kenneth Murray, 59 years. It also lay on the surface of the shiny black footwear of those who gathered to pay their last respects to a local hotelier who had been a good friend to many. Tessa Murray's shoulders slumped as, huddled under an outsized umbrella, she clung for support to her son, Alexander, and her daughter, Alison, as they said their final farewell to a loving husband and father.

Back at the Montpelier House Hotel, home to family for thirty years, Alison stood on the top step of the flagstone staircase that led down to the garden. The voices coming from the assembled mourners inside the Caithness stone villa were at times loud and high-pitched and the drizzle had turned into a downpour. Alison watched as fat raindrops dripped from the tips of the garden brolly onto the polished curves of the garden furniture that sat in what was her favourite corner of the garden, furniture her father had lovingly crafted from recycled herring barrels. Tears mingled with the rain on her face as she recalled the vital part the old scarred table and chairs had played in the lives of the Murray family. The scene of many celebrations, it was also where life-changing family decisions had been made. It was there, on the day she left home to take up her place at college, her father had said, 'When you return, Alison, you and I will follow my dream and revamp the Montpelier.' Alison smiled as she recalled his words and the way his face lit up when he spoke.

She had harboured a dream for the best part of a decade, a dream that envisaged finishing high school followed by a college course in hotel management. Fresh from graduating in the top five per cent of her class, the twenty-three-year old Alison couldn't wait to get going.

What was it she'd said to her best friend, Lucy, just a few weeks ago?

'I have the perfect job waiting for me, the perfect life.'

The Montpelier House Hotel had been part of Wick since Alison's grandfather, John Ross, who'd managed to sustain a living as a licensed grocer over a period of twenty three years when Wick was a *'dry town'*, decided in 1947 to take over the old hotel that perched on a slope overlooking the river. Other, grander establishments had come and gone, bringing various nouvelle cuisine and chic modern style to the area, but only three hotels remained in the town. One of which was Montpelier House, the big rambling Georgian villa, crammed with shabby antiques, that was hell to heat and had managed to stay only more or less solvent in the thirty years since Alison's parents had taken it over.

Newly married Tessa and Kenneth Murray had thrown themselves into running the place. Although Tessa had been born to the trade, Kenneth, who up until his marriage had been a rep for one of the big whisky distillers, had little experience of running a hotel. Between them they'd just about managed, and over three decades and two children later the Montpelier was still there. It featured in guide books, in the family-run category, as the sort of place where guests could feel they were visiting a friend's large, old fashioned, comfortably down-at-heel home rather than a hotel. There were ten bedrooms, a dining room, a public bar and a ballroom where small, intimate wedding receptions were held.

The hotel was the same as it had always been. It was Wick that had changed over the years. Now one of the most challenging wind and wave power centres in the country, property prices had rocketed and other hotel owners were always trying to set up shop.

Two months had passed since Kenneth Murray's untimely death, two months that saw his daughter roll up her sleeves and work alongside her mother in the hotel and doing a very good job, as well as bringing fresh ideas and new methods of hotel management to the running of the Montpelier.

Crossing the bridge over the Wick river, Alison's teeth chattered as she turned her collar up against a shower of hailstones. Hailstones in May. Alison smiled a wistful, little smile. It's what her grandfather used to call the 'May Gobs'. She thrust cold hands into the pockets of her jacket and for the umpteenth time that day, mulled over her decision to turn down the job as part of the management team at the Dubai Dusit. Her friend Lucy had said she needed her head examined and as needle-like spicules of ice attacked her face, Alison was beginning to think her friend was right.

The agent who recruited for the Dusit chain clearly thought so, too. Alison had spoken to him on the phone after getting the job offer in the post.

'You were so keen and enthusiastic,' he said, his tone revealing his irritation.

'I'm really sorry. I didn't mean to waste your time.'

'Well, you did.'

'Not intentionally.' Alison swallowed over a lump in her throat. 'It... it's... just something suddenly cropped up.' She hesitated. 'You know I come from a hotel background? Well...

77

well... there's a good reason for me to stay at home and work with my family right now.' Alison fought back the tears. 'My father died.'

There was a short pause at the other end of the phone.

'I'm very sorry to hear that, Ms Murray. Sorry for your loss. We were all very impressed with you at your interview, and wish you all the very best for the future.'

'Thank you,' said Alison, in a voice tinged with regret. Instinct told her that the Dubai Dusit would have been a wonderful place to work, but she couldn't bring herself to give up on her family and abandon her mother.

Her brother, Alexander, who had no interest in the hotel except to discuss its finances had, at the age of twenty-five, been given a ten per cent share in the business.

'Twenty-five is ridiculous,' said Alison 'It's so far off it's almost Victorian.' She was eighteen when she heard about the scheme and realised she was years away from being part of it.

As Alison took the path along the riverside, she knew she had a fight on her hands, but she was determined to drag the Montpelier and what was left of her family into the twenty-first century before the hotel went under.

The shower had passed, watery sunshine peeped from behind the clouds. She quickened her step as she passed the boarded-up building that had been the most recent competition to the Montpelier – the Plum Palace, so nicknamed because of its abundance of mirrors and lavish plum-coloured velvet furnishings.

Alison smiled as she remembered what her father had to say about it. He had checked it out on the q.t. and was able to report back that the breakfasts were bad – continental instead of the good solid fry-up that most people wanted. He had also found out that the owner seemed more interested in having the place photographed in style magazines than attending to the daily routine of a hotel. Kenneth Murray thought that its closure after only a year was reassurance that people liked solid home cooking and a cosy atmosphere instead of flashy style and expensive new furnishings.

Given that nothing at the Montpelier had been updated since she was a child, Alison sighed and thought this was all just as well, but she didn't say so.

Alison's mother said that this was proof the Montpelier was part and parcel of Wick. 'People drive from other parts of the county to join the locals for Sunday lunch and book up months in advance for Christmas Day.'

'Yes,' said Alexander, between mouthfuls of homemade shortbread. 'This place could be a little gold mine with everything that's going on at the harbour and marina. And what's the point of shelling out lots of money to upgrade the heating system just because the plumber reckoned that the pipes were beyond their use-by date?'

Alison was the only one to sound a note of warning. There was passion in her voice as she urged her family to think about refurbishing. 'Caithness and Wick in particular are going through a period of renewed prosperity. The time is right. It would be very easy for a hotel like this to slide into the doldrums because of a lack of vision.'

Her father had been the only one to agree with her.

'Alison's right in what she's saying. Big, modern hotels are generally owned by corporations who can afford to invest, but are intent on keeping an impersonal eye on the bottom line. Smaller establishments like this have something special to offer as boutique hotels with high standards and facilities, yet maintaining the intimacy of a small hotel.'

'Yes, indeed,' said Alison. 'But if standards slip and money isn't spent, your small hotel can go from having every bed occupied to being empty every night very quickly.'

The memory of that conversation was on Alison's mind as she walked up the lane that led to the entrance of the Montpelier. She walked through the front door and did what one of her favourite lecturers used to tell the students to do – imagine they were guests arriving at the hotel and see what it felt like. Alison tried to see the hotel with a dispassionate eye.

The flowers that had only one day left in them yesterday still stood on the big hall table. No one had got round to changing the water. The clear vase showed water murky and green and it gave the hall the aroma of bad eggs. The cushions on the big armchairs in front of the fireplace still bore the imprints of whoever had sat in them last and a newspaper was squashed into a corner of one of them. Alison didn't have to imagine what any self-respecting guest's reaction would be if they'd travelled to the Montpelier hoping for warmth and welcome to be greeted by all this. Alison saw the hotel with new eyes. The place was tired, a dump. It badly needed a total revamp.

Alison's mother sat in the tiny alcove in the kitchen where an old church pew had been wedged to provide a seat where people rushing around cooking and serving could take a rest and a cup of tea. Alison loved this corner, it was where she and her brother had played and done much of their homework while their parents spun past as they cleaned and cooked. It had been a fun way to grow up.

Her thoughts took a wavering step into the future. Her children would play in the hotel, she decided. She'd want them to enjoy their birthright the way she had. Of course, that was years and years off. She didn't even have a man in her life at the moment.

It was from her father that Alison had learned her love of business and, hopefully, her skill with people. Kenneth Murray had a way with people that made them comfortable in his company. The perfect gift for a hotelier.

'How are you, Mum? Okay?' Alison put an arm around her mother's shoulder. Tessa looked up from the magazine she was studying. 'I'm good. But you look frozen to the bone.' She patted the cushion by her side. 'Come over here by the Aga. Was that hailstones I heard rattling off the window? And here I was thinking about a shopping trip to find some nice lightweight clothes for your trip to the Emirates.'

Alison lowered her eyes. She hadn't told her mother about turning down the job in Dubai.

She studied the woman sitting next to her. Since she'd started wearing the spindly, gilt bifocals, Tessa looked so much older. For years, Mum had been so young and lively, with the same nut-brown curls as her own. But suddenly her hair was almost white and the lines around her blue eyes were so deep they looked as if they'd been carved with a razor knife. Her hands were misshapen with arthritis, the knuckles on both swollen, and where she'd once made an effort with pearly nail varnishes, her nails were bare. Her mother missed her husband and she was worn down by work. Alison felt a surge of remorse that she hadn't noticed this before.

The back door opened and Alexander and his wife, Thea, arrived in a whirl of cold wind and Hugo Boss – a perfume Alison had once liked and now hated because Thea seemed to wear a pint of it.

'Hello, just thought we'd drop in to say hi,' said Thea, immaculate in jodhpurs, hacking jacket and full make-up.

'Thea's just back from a gymkhana and didn't feel like cooking so we came into town to cadge a couple of free meals.'

Alexander had married Thea, a farmer's daughter, and now managed her father's farm on the other side of the county.

'How's my favourite daughter-in-law?' said Tessa, planting a kiss on Thea's cheek. 'Sit down, folks. Chef's got some lovely sea bass and I'm sure if you ask her nicely, she'll rustle up some chips to go with it.'

'Great,' Thea sighed as she sat down in the comfiest corner of the pew and flicked through an interior design magazine, while Alexander scavenged in the main part of the kitchen for a snack. Having found a fistful of almond cookies, he squeezed in beside his wife, who had come to the page Alison's mum had been looking at.

'That's nice,' said Alexander, munching.

'Isn't it?' said Tessa. 'Alison wonders if we could do something like that here.'

Thea raised perfectly shaped eyebrows. 'But impossible to copy,' she said. 'It would cost a fortune.'

'You think?' said Alison.

'For goodness sake, Alison, didn't they teach you anything in college? Paint effects are expensive. Or maybe you were planning to do it yourself.'

The first feelings of anger stirred in Alison's veins.

'As a matter of fact, I was. The whole place needs work and this is one option that wouldn't cost too much. We weren't full over Easter and it's about time we all faced facts and did something about it. We don't want to lose the place, do we?'

She could sense rather than see her mother and brother stiffen at these words. They didn't answer. Alison felt her anger rising. They were doing what they always did; deliberately avoiding any mention of the hotel's shortcomings – ostriches with their heads in the sand.

'I think your mother and brother know what they're doing,' Thea said.

Alison's plans to be diplomatic took a dive. 'So a degree in hotel management is a waste of time and money and I know nothing about running a hotel?'

'You said it, not me,' said Thea, a self-satisfied smirk on her face.

'Please don't argue,' said Tessa.

'All I'm saying is that the hotel's in trouble and nobody's talking about it,' Alison argued. She stopped when she saw the looked that passed between her mother and her brother.

'Have you any steak, chef?' called Alexander. 'I'm starving.'

'Chef doesn't have time to whip up private meals for you,' Alison snapped. 'You've been here four times in the past week for dinner. Can neither of you cook?'

Thea looked daggers at her sister-in-law. 'I'm busy with my horses, my livery stable.'

'Lots of women work, but they don't expect their husband's family business to dole out money to support them,' Alison said, taking the gloves off. She knew her parents had supplemented Alexander's income with handouts. Handouts that Alexander felt were entirely his due.

'It's a loan,' snarled Thea

'Four loans in the past two years?'

'It's none of your business.'

'It's my business when the hotel profits are being siphoned off into your pockets,' said Alison

'Don't, please, Alison,' Tessa pleaded.

'Yeah, who do you think you are?' said Alexander, remembering his duty as a husband after a dig in the ribs from Thea. 'Apologise.'

Alison was about to say she had no intentions of apologising when every word she'd said was true. Her mother interrupted. 'Yes, apologise, Alison.'

Stunned, she spun around to look at her mother.

'For telling the truth?'

'We don't have big rows in this family,' Tessa went on. 'It doesn't help. Please apologise to Thea.'

Alison bristled. She felt betrayed. Her mother rarely interfered in squabbles and it was hardly a family secret that she and Thea didn't get on. She loved and respected her mother but Tessa was wrong about this. She was being punished for telling the truth.

Alison knew why her mother hated rows. Alison's grandmother had been what her daughter euphemistically called 'fiery' and Tessa had grown up watching her parents face each other, screaming insults.

Alison knew she'd inherited her grandmother's passion, but hopefully, not her harsh tongue.

'You're right,' she said calmly, glancing towards Thea. 'I'm sorry if I upset you, Mum. I'm going for a walk.'

Alison went and sat where she often sat when she was upset – down at the corner of the garden where the old table and chairs were. As Alison ran her hand over the old furniture, she noticed not for the first time that it was in need of a coat of varnish.

Over the years, some of the hotel's brides and grooms had found this secluded spot and been photographed there. For that reason alone, the barrel-shaped garden set should have been taken care of, but nobody listened to her when she said it. And they probably never would, she realised with a jolt.

Idly, she picked at a blister on the surface of the table. Several creepy crawlies fell out. Feeling like a murderer, Alison tried to replace the bubble of wood but it wouldn't stick.

'Sorry, boys,' she said to the insects who made a rapid exit onto the stony ground at her feet. 'You've lost your home and the Murrays will lose theirs too.'

Five days later, Alison closed the garden gate behind her. She'd enjoyed her trip to her friend's wedding and the time away had given her a chance to think things through. A faint pink tinge still lingered about the edges of the sky. The best time of day to appreciate the Montpelier, she thought as the setting sun reflected the elegance of the blue-black stone and the yellow roses that clung to the wall by the door.

'Welcome home, Alison. You're just in time.' Alexander put his arm around her shoulders and drew her close. Alexander was so much more like the brother she'd grown up with when Thea wasn't around. Calluses on the palm of his hand rubbed against the fabric of her top. Why hadn't she noticed them before? Those and the streaks of grey at his temples, the weather-beaten face, with deep lines around the corners of faded blue eyes that made him look ten years older than his thirty years. Could it be that she'd been so wrapped up in her own interests that she'd failed to see what was going on with those closest to her? She had to make more of an effort with him, she thought. It was stupid to let her dislike of Thea ruin her relationship with her brother.

'Just in time for what?' said Alison.

'Champagne.'

'Champagne?'

Alexander led her to the garden table where her mother sat, a glass of the sparkling liquid in front of her. 'Great, we hoped you'd be here soon,' Tessa said, getting up to hug Alison.

'Hi, Mum. What's going on?'

'We're celebrating,' Tessa said cheerfully.

Alison looked at Alexander but he avoided her eyes as he poured her a drink.

'Celebrating what?' Alison's voice caught in her throat.

'We've sold the Montpelier,' Alexander said. 'And it's a fabulous offer. Twenty per cent more than the estate agent thought we would get. *Twenty per cent*,' he repeated.

Her brother words sounded as if they were coming from a dark, bad dream in her head.

'What? Why?' she stammered.

'It was such a good offer, Alison,' said Tessa, a note of apology in her voice. 'I know it's a bit sudden, but...'

'The decision's been made and it's final,' Alexander interrupted. 'As soon as the developer heard we might be putting the place on the market, he jumped, we closed the deal this afternoon.'

Alison ignored him and looked at her mother who, eyes lowered, fingered the stem of her glass. Alison willed her to tell her it was all a mistake; that they hadn't made a decision to sell her home. But her mother kept silent.

'It's a good move financially,' said Alexander, looking first at his mother, then Alison. 'For all of us.'

'Mum?' Alison sat down next to her mother. For the first time Tessa looked up into her daughter's eyes. 'It's true, Alison,' she said. 'I'm tired and I can't do this anymore without your father.'

'You didn't have to sell. I would have run it for you.'

'You run it?' said Alexander, blustering the way he did when there was any kind of disagreement. 'Get real, Alison. You're just out of college. What hope would you have of turning this place around. Anyway, the deal's done. This is the best move for all of us. The developer wants to turn the place into accommodation for guys coming and going offshore. If they're held up for any reason at the helipad, they stay here. It was always going to happen. We did the right thing.'

'What do you mean *we* did the right thing?' said Alison. 'Where was I when all this *we* stuff was going on? When you were making decisions that affected me?'

'Calm down, little sis,' said Alexander.

Alison rounded on him like a tigress, eyes blazing. Don't you 'little sis', me, you slacker.'

'I'm no slacker, Alison,' said Alexander. I work hard on the farm and don't forget, from the time I left school I worked in this hotel. I was pulling pints from the day I was old enough to do so. I don't have a college education, but I've got enough sense to see this place is a millstone that never made any money till now.'

'Money!' Alison spat the word out. 'Is that all you care about? You'd throw a lifetime's work away so that your wife can shop till she drops?' Alison knew by the look on her brother's face that she'd hit a nerve. Bloody Thea! There was no doubt in Alison's mind that her sister-in-law was behind this. Could the property developer who'd been sniffing around be the same one who shot clay pigeons with Alexander and dropped his girls complete with tack and riding attire at Thea's stables every Saturday morning?

'Don't talk to your brother like that,' begged Tessa. 'Please, love, it's not worth fighting over. It's only a business. We can't let it destroy us.'

'You don't understand, do you?' Alison looked from her mother to her brother. 'It was Dad's dream and this is more than a hotel to me – it's something else, it's in my blood.'

'Don't be so bloody dramatic,' snapped Alexander. 'You'll be telling us next that's why you turned down the job in Dubai.'

'You turned down the job in Dubai?' Tessa stretched an arm across the table, took Alison's hand in her own. 'But, why, Alison? It was a great opportunity for you. A chance to see another part of the world, a chance to shake off the twenty-four-seven grind of running a small family hotel.'

'I turned it down so I could be here and change things.' She faced her mother but the fire had gone out of her, replaced by a crushing feeling of defeat. 'I love you, Mum. I had hoped you'd have faith in me to bring this place round but you didn't. I'm just the kid in the family.'

'And you're acting like one,' snapped Alexander. 'Listen, Alison, if you don't like it, get the hell out.'

Alison ignored him and looked at her mother. 'Is that what you want?' Her mother looked jittery, as she always did during family rows.

Alison felt the balance of her life lying in the palm of her mother's hand, but she knew her mother had to let go. Her parents had worked hard and it would have been lovely if their children could have taken over the hotel. Her dream was shattered but the deed was done and they had to move on. Alison might have had the fire of her grandmother, but she had something else that Muriel Ross had always lacked – she had enormous loyalty. She had to support her mother. *I hate what you're doing but I'll support you.* The words were in her head, ready to be spoken when Alexander cut in.

'Are you going to stay, Alison, get your share of the money, or stand by your convictions and walk off?'

Alison waited for her mother to tell Alexander to back off. Say something like. 'We'll work it out.' Waited for Alexander to hug her and say, he was sorry. But nobody moved or said a word.

Up to that point there had been hope. The awful silence of her family dashed that hope. Their minds were made up.

'Stand by my convictions, of course,' said Alison.

She stood up and straightened her back. There was no way she'd let them see how devastated she felt. 'I never thought you'd do something so awful behind my back. I thought I was part of this family but I can see that I'm not. So the only thing I can do is leave.'

She could hear muffled sobs coming from her mother, but didn't look in her direction. Instead, she gripped the edge of the table. She was shaking although she tried her best to hide it. 'I'd hate to stay here and watch them tear our home apart. I couldn't face it.' Dark clouds gathered overhead and tears welled up in her eyes. Before turning towards the staircase that led to the door of the hotel, Alison ran her hand over the curved surface of one of the garden chairs. 'You're making a big mistake,' was all she said.

Read more by Margaret Mackay.

https://www.amazon.co.uk/No-More-Secrets-Lies-ebook

A Cry from Below

John Knowles

Jessica Palmer hauled the Triumph Speed Triple onto its stand and unzipped her leather jacket. Wavy red hair cascaded down her back as she removed her crash helmet. Jess loved her motorcycle. She also loved living in the far north of Scotland. For her, Caithness was perfect for motorcycling, with its quiet, open roads and magnificent scenery. Jess adored painting, too, and since freeing herself from a tedious nine to five job in the city, she could now pursue her dream of becoming a successful artist. Caithness, with its wide-open skies and beautiful sandy beaches, seemed the perfect place to make her home. The North Highlands were certainly a far cry from the hustle and bustle of her native Manchester.

It was a beautiful sunny spring day and the ride from Reay to John O'Groats had been exhilarating. The roads were still reasonably clear of traffic. The annual cavalcade of camper vans had yet to dawdle their way north. As a result Jessica had been able to give the Triumph a bit of a blast. She looked longingly across the Pentland Firth towards Stroma, as she'd done many times before. The island fascinated her, especially as it had been uninhabited for years. She desperately wanted to go over there to explore and take photographs. Jess often imagined what it would've been like living on such a small island nestled between mainland Scotland and Orkney.

If she could get some good photographs, she could use these as a guide for potential paintings.

Sandy Mackay stroked the bristles of his prominent chin. He was a slender man who, she estimated, was in his mid-seventies. Short greying hair lay untidily above a weather-beaten face. His brown eyes were soft and kind. 'I sometimes take folk over for an hour or two, but never to camp overnight,' he said firmly. 'I'm sorry lass, it's all about health and safety you see. You know what it's like these days.'

Jess lowered her eyes, signalling her disappointment.

'Stroma looks perfect subject matter for a painting or two.'

'Ah, you're an artist are you, lass?' Sandy said, raising an eyebrow.

'It's a hobby really, but I'd like to make a living out of it if I could. Isn't there any way you could make an exception, just this once?'

Sandy pulled a packet of cigarettes from his top pocket, extracted the last one, and placed it between his lips. He crushed the empty packet and tossed it into a nearby bin. Lighting the cigarette, he took a long deep drag.

'Trouble is, lass, if I let you camp on the island, they'll all want to do it. Stroma's tranquillity would be ruined. Besides, Stroma's a haven for nesting sea birds at this time of the year and I don't want them disturbing. You do understand, don't you, lassie?'

'Yes, I suppose so.' Jessica stared across the flat, calm water of the Pentland Firth towards the island. 'Okay, how about letting me go over for the day, just me?'

Taking the cigarette from his mouth Sandy gave her a sanguine smile, before flicking the ash onto the ground. 'It wouldn't be worth my while taking just one person across lass. Diesel's expensive and my old wee boat gets through it like a flock of seagulls would through a fish supper.'

Jess chuckled at his humorous analogy. 'Oh well never mind, I guess I'll just tag along with the next group you take across. It won't have the same ambience, but hey ho, beggars can't be choosers, I suppose.' Sandy took another drag on his cigarette, inhaling the smoke deeply. He sighed, letting the smoke drift out from between his lips.

'Of course, were you to donate one of your paintings of the island to me, maybe I could make an exception. No tents though, I'd be picking you up later on in the day, you understand.'

'Yes, yes, thank you! I'd be delighted to do a painting for you.'

'Okay then, but let's keep this secret. I don't want others expecting a similar trip. This is a one off, you understand.'

Sandy and his boat were patiently waiting as Jess swung her Triumph down the slip road towards the Gills Bay jetty. Parking close to the terminal building she dismounted and pulled out her camera and a compact tripod.

'Hello, what a lovely morning,' she said, smiling.

Sandy grinned and pretended to pipe her aboard. 'Good morning, lass. You all set to go across then?'

'Oh yes, can't wait.'

He held out a steadying arm as she boarded the vessel.

'It should be a good crossing today, all being well.'

The diesel engine roared into life as they pulled away from the jetty. Thick clouds of black smoke belched into clear early morning sky.

A multitude of seabirds swooped and soared above them as *Song of the Sea* ploughed through the undulating water. The rhythmic beat of the engine was almost hypnotic. Jess sat at the bow, the wind blowing through her hair. Closing her eyes, she breathed the ozone deep into her lungs. This was the life.

Twenty minutes later *Song of the Sea* entered the tiny harbour on the southern tip of the island. Sandy skilfully guided the boat into the harbour and threw a mooring rope onto the jetty. He leapt ashore, like a man half his age. With the boat secured he helped Jess up the short flight of steps leading to the quayside.

91

'I'll be back to pick you up at eight tonight, okay? Make sure you're here on time.'

'I'll be here at eight and thanks, I really appreciate this.'

'That's alright lass, but like I said, keep this to yourself.'

She grinned and turned to climb the hill that led away from the harbour. With the chug of the engine fading away, Jess suddenly felt very alone. All she had for company now was the wind, the sheep and thousands of nesting seabirds.

The path soon joined a rough track that lead past numerous ruined buildings. In the distance she could see the old kirk that stood in the heart of what had been the village. Apart from the lighthouse, the kirk was the tallest building on the island and could be clearly seen from the mainland. Approaching the kirk, she stopped, taking the rucksack from her shoulders. The glassless windows of ruined buildings all around her suddenly made her feel uneasy. It was as if unseen eyes were watching her. The wind was picking up now as she took her camera out to take a couple of photos. A feeling of melancholy swept over her as she walked between the remains of the cottages. As she approached the old kirk, to her shock she saw a woman standing in the doorway of a whitewashed cottage. Who on earth is this, she thought. A sudden feeling of resentment coursed through her. Sandy had promised she'd be alone on the island. As she fumbled for the camera's lens cap, it slipped through her fingers and fell to the ground.

'Damn it,' she whispered to herself, bending to pick it up. By the time she raised her eyes, the woman had gone. Looking all around she could see no sign of anyone.

'I saw her, I know I saw her.' She spoke the words out loud. Puzzled, she continued up the track.

An old red telephone box stood outside the kirk, its windows smashed, green algae discolouring its flaking red framework. Stroma was fantastic, so photogenic! Jess was in her element, photographing the old kirk and telephone box from every conceivable angle.

The image of the woman standing in the cottage doorway suddenly wheedled its way back into her mind. She wondered if she'd imagined it or whether it had been a trick of the light. The dwelling was only about a hundred yards away and it had somehow survived the ravages of the Caithness climate. Within a couple of minutes, she was standing outside the front door, its blue paint flaking, exposing grey weathered wood beneath. Grubby net curtains hung limply behind fully glazed square window frames. The property almost looked habitable. Curiosity soon got the better of her. She turned the handle and gently pushed on the door. Rusty hinges groaned, as if in mortal pain. As her eyes adjusted to the dimness inside, she could see that there were two rooms. A damp musty odour filled her nostrils as she edged in. On the kitchen table an old box of cornflakes lay on its side, a tin mug and dish rusting beside it. It was almost as if the owner had left in a hurry never to return. She peered into the second room, which was considerably smaller. A curtained window let in a minuscule amount of light. In the far corner was a box-bed, its pillow and blankets still neat and tidy. A sudden feeling of sadness swept over her. This did not feel like a happy house. It was as if she expected the owner to suddenly walk in and catch her trespassing. She was however, determined to get some photographs of the place. Nervously she fumbled with the camera's exposure controls.

Having taken a series of shots, she decided she really didn't want to be in that cottage any longer.

Re-joining the track she walked past a modest war memorial and down towards the sea. On the headland, a rather magnificent lighthouse looked out across the Pentland Firth towards Orkney. Black menacing clouds were gathering on the horizon and the wind had become stronger. A sudden feeling of urgency overcame her. Should she return to the old cottage or take a chance with the weather? She'd take a chance, conscious that there was so much of the island still to see. The track sloped gently downwards towards the sea, which she figured was about a five-minute walk away. Beneath her feet patches of old tarmac showed through the rough track, indicating a former metalled road.

Gazing out to sea she spotted the swirling waters of the Swelkie, a notorious giant whirlpool. She'd heard tales about the Swelkie from local fishermen. These tales told of small boats that strayed too close to its menacing core, never to be seen again. A shiver ran down her spine as she thought of the poor mariners sucked down into the heart of the whirlpool. Capturing a few photographs of the swirling maelstrom, she carried on with her walk around the coastline.

As she walked, her mind wandered back to her previous life in Manchester. All those lost hours spent sitting in motorway traffic jams. Stroma was like a different planet compared to that. If only her friends back home could see her now. She gave a small sigh of contentment as she strode out towards the island's western coast and her next photographic target, 'The Gloup.'

A collapsed sea cave, the Gloup was basically a gigantic deep chasm. Way below, a brutal sea smashed relentlessly against the rocks. A feeling of vertigo overtook her as she stood there, two metres from the edge. Some unseen force seemed to entice her towards the cliff top, even though she knew to fall would be fatal. Despite her vertigo, Jess couldn't resist the temptation to take some photographs and she fired off a dozen frames of the Gloup before backing away.

A sudden rumble in her stomach reminded her that she hadn't eaten anything for hours. Looking at her watch she was shocked to see that it was already one thirty. She rummaged in her rucksack and retrieved the lunch box she'd packed earlier that morning. She pulled the lid off, but to her horror her sandwiches were coated in a thick green mould. Maggots crawled out from between the slices of bread. Instinctively, she dropped the box, the sandwiches scattering onto the grass. When she looked again, the sandwiches were as fresh as the moment she made them. She rubbed her forehead, trying to make sense of what she thought she'd seen. Although hungry, she wasn't going to eat sandwiches that had been on the ground. Picking up the now empty box, she pushed it back into her rucksack. It was then that she noticed a green slimy gunge floating in her water bottle. Turning away she retched. When she looked again, to her amazement the water was as clear as crystal. Now she was beginning to question her sanity.

The sorrowful cry of a gull suddenly invaded her mind. It sounded more like the cry of a child. A large raindrop landed on her head, then another and before she could pull up her hood it was raining. Stuffing the bottle back into her rucksack, she decided to head back towards the ram-shackled ruins of the village. She'd shelter in the old house she'd found earlier, until the rain stopped. Sandy Mackay wouldn't be across for another six and a half hours.

Raindrops hammered down on the slated roof of the old cottage, as Jess sat on a rocking chair beside the window. The wind was now howling, rain beating against the windowpanes. Looking out, Jess saw the figure of a woman dressed in a black dress standing motionless on the path.

It's her, it's that woman again, she thought, getting up take a better look. The woman stood motionless, seeming to hover a few inches above the track. Despite the torrential downpour Jess felt compelled to fetch the poor soul in. By the time she'd opened the cottage door the figure was fading away. Within seconds the woman had vanished.

Frowning, she turned and ran back into the cottage, slamming the door behind her. Her gasp of horror was palpable as her heart leapt into her mouth. In the rocking chair she'd vacated only seconds earlier sat the young woman.

Jess froze, her mouth as dry as the Sahara desert, and her hands were trembling. The woman was clothed in a black dress with a dark blue woollen shawl draped across her shoulders. Her face was white and smooth, melancholy steel-grey eyes stared out at her. Jess tried to speak, but the words refused to come. After what seemed like an eternity her speech returned.

'Hello,' Jess said nervously. 'I'm sorry; I didn't realise this was your home. I'll go if you like.'

The figure made no reply. Suddenly the chair started to rock to and fro.

Dredging up every morsel of courage, Jess edged closer to the figure. She was within touching distance now and tentatively extended a hand. Instantly the woman started to fade and within seconds Jess was staring at an empty, but still rocking, chair. The rocking ceased abruptly and all was silent. Only the hammering of rain on the window and the wind howling around the eaves could be heard.

No, this wasn't happening, was it? She tried to convince herself that she'd fallen asleep in the cottage and that the woman was part of some crazy dream. Jess glanced at her watch and to her amazement noticed it was a quarter past seven. 'It can't be that late surely,' she said under her breath. Somewhere she'd lost three or four hours. The daylight was starting to fade, hastened by the atrocious weather. Jess figured it was a fifteen-minute walk to the jetty. She'd wait until the rain eased off a little and then make her way to the harbour. Sandy Mackay and his boat couldn't come too soon. Half an hour later Jess hauled open the door and stepped out into the howling gale. The wind clawed mercilessly at her hair and clothes as she battled against it. Approaching the jetty she looked out across the turbulent waves of the Pentland Firth towards the mainland. There was no sign of Sandy's boat. Maybe he'd been delayed or had taken an alternative route across the firth. The cold was seeping deep into her bones now, making her shiver. She pulled up her jacket collar and crouched behind a stone wall. Retrieving her rucksack, she slung it over her shoulder and pulled up the hood of her coat.

Sandy cursed the weather as he tried to keep his boat on an even keel. The speed at which the storm had struck had taken him by surprise. Now he was torn between turning back to the mainland or battling on to Stroma. The swell was making it almost impossible to steer a steady course. Gigantic waves smashed against the bows, the salty spray slowly filling the hull with seawater. Sandy turned on the bilge pump, before frantically wrestling with the boat's wheel. Ploughing on, the *Song of the Sea* was now within a few hundred yards of shore, but struggling to maintain her intended course. Suddenly the big diesel engine coughed, spluttered, and then belched out a plume of black acrid smoke, before dying.

'Oh for heaven's sake, now what?' he said as he desperately pulled on the starter. The engine turned over but refused to fire. The *Song of the Sea* was now drifting aimlessly, blown off course. With the bilge pump inoperable, he had to use a bucket to bail out the water. He'd have to radio for help. It was then that he noticed the wet and smashed radio.

'Damn, that's all I need, no bloody radio!' Ahead he could see the menacing outline of jagged rocks, protruding from the water. If he hit them, they'd rip the bottom clean out of his boat. He frantically pulled on the starter again.

'Come on you bastard, start!' he cried, the words lost in the gale. Grabbing hold of the boat's wheel, Sandy pulled it hard to the right. To his relief the boat responded and moved away from the rocks. The problem was he'd drifted past the only harbour on the island. He had to keep on trying to restart the engine. Suddenly the boat swung violently to the left setting it on a course that would push it west along the northern coast of the island. A wide shaft of luminosity swept across the raging maelstrom from Stroma's lighthouse. It was then that Sandy spotted the swirling, chaotic mass of water straight ahead. The dreaded Swelkie whirlpool that had claimed many lives over the centuries. Sandy pulled and pulled on the starter, praying that the engine would fire. If it didn't, he and his boat would be lost.

Jess's boots slipped on the muddy track. Leaving the harbour behind, she made her way back towards Stroma village.

Suddenly she felt the wet gritty taste of earth in her mouth. Thick brown mud oozed between her outstretched fingers as she lay helplessly on the ground. A sharp stabbing pain shot up her right leg when she tried to stand. Crying out, she collapsed. In the fading light. She must have inadvertently strayed off the track, and tripped over a rusty piece of farm machinery.

'Sod it, my bloody ankle; I've twisted my bloody ankle.' Pulling her sock down, she rubbed the sore foot. Now she'd done it, stranded on Stroma in appalling weather and unable to walk properly. Then she remembered she'd brought her tripod with her. She could use the legs as a walking pole. With the tripod fully extended, Jess hauled herself upright and hobbled the few feet back onto the track. By the time she'd reached the old kirk, she was exhausted and wet through. The doors of the church were hanging off their hinges, allowing her access. She would shelter there and figure out what to do next. Her ankle throbbed and she felt sick.

Pulling her mobile phone from her pocket she noticed there was no signal. Her heart sank. Suddenly she heard a faint rustling coming from above her head. Someone or something was in here with her. Activating the phone's built in torch; Jess scanned the walls and ceiling, but saw nothing. A sudden flapping of wings and then a rush of air across her face startled her. A large bird had swooped down brushing the top of her head before exciting the building. Jess's heart was thumping frantically as if it would burst free from her ribcage. She stumbled across to a pew and sat down, taking the weight off her injured foot. It wasn't long before she drifted into a fitful sleep.

When she next opened her eyes, she couldn't remember where she was. A sharp pain shot up her leg as she tried to stand up, making her collapse back down into the pew. Now she remembered. Outside the wind had dropped and it was no longer raining. Suddenly she thought she heard a noise. It was so faint it was almost inaudible. There it was again. It sounded like a child crying.

'I've got to be imaging it or losing my mind,' she said. In the darkness something rolled across a flat surface and fell to the ground with a clatter, making her jump. The beam from her torch revealed an empty tin. She could just about pick out the words, 'Cow and Gate Milk Food, Full Cream', printed on the side. Baby milk. What was an old tin of baby milk doing in a church? she thought. She had to get out of this place. With an almighty effort she heaved herself up onto one leg, using her trusty tripod and hobbled to the double doors that led outside.

Dragging herself along the track, she eventually reached the cottage again. There was smoke spilling into the evening sky from the chimney. The woman must be real, she hadn't imagined her, she thought. When she reached the front door she knocked. There was no reply. She knocked a second time, but still no response. Gingerly she turned the door handle and pushed open the door. The house was in darkness. 'Hello, is anyone at home?' There was no reply. Scanning the room with her torch, she could see that the cottage was empty. Shivering, she suddenly realised there was no fire burning in the grate. But she'd seen smoke from the chimney!

What with ghostly apparitions, maggot infested sandwiches and now this, Jess was convinced she must be going mad. Sitting down in the rocking chair exhausted, she again drifted into a restless slumber. In a distant corner of her mind Jess could hear the plaintive cry of a baby. It disturbed her; a feeling of intense melancholy totally overwhelmed her. Whose baby was it and why was it crying? She woke with a start, the coldness of the room, bringing her back to reality. Suddenly from the other room, Jess heard a noise. It sounded like something had fallen onto the stone floor. She shrank back into the chair clutching her coat tightly around her shivering body. What on earth was that? she thought, wondering whether to put herself through the pain of shuffling over to investigate. Curiosity prevailed and she heaved herself upright and hobbled across to the doorway.

Pushing open the door, she peeped nervously into the darkness. She could just about make out the outline of the box-bed but nothing else. Switching on her torch, Jess recoiled in horror. The headless body of a doll lay on the flags; a few inches away, its head was gently rocking to and fro. Jess stared transfixed as the head slowly lost momentum. The eyes were missing, making the deep dark sockets look terrifyingly creepy. She wondered why the porcelain hadn't shattered. It was then she heard the faint cry of a baby once again. Where was the baby, and more to the point, where was its mother?

'No, no, this isn't happening. It can't be happening,' she whimpered. She wanted to run, run as fast as she could, away from the sound of the crying child, but she felt frozen to the spot. Besides, with a twisted ankle she wasn't going to run anywhere. A mixture of emotions swept over her. She was scared, confused but most of all tired and weary. Jess realized that until Sandy Mackay came for her, she had to sit tight. Pressing the palms of her hands over her ears, she tried to block out the sound of the crying child. What had started out as a day full of excitement and adventure had turned into a living nightmare.

She had to get a grip; after all she was a forty year old woman. She had to deal with the situation. Now she'd heard the baby three times and in different places. A gentle tapping on the window made her jump. Hobbling over to it, she looked out into the blackness beyond. There was nobody there.

The outer edge of the whirlpool was now less than a hundred yards away. Sandy knew that if he didn't start the motor now he and his boat would be sucked into the rotating body of water and swallowed. In desperation he pulled the starter one last time. The battery was almost flat. All of a sudden there was a cough, then a splutter, and the engine finally fired. Sandy revved the engine, anxious not to let it stall. Although not a religious man, he found himself thanking God for saving his mortal soul.

Looking through the glass, Sandy saw someone inside the cottage asleep in the chair. It was too dark to make out who.

The rap on the door made Jess jump.

Sandy Mackay didn't wait for a reply and walked inside.

'Oh, it's you, Mr Mackay, thank God! I was beginning to think you weren't coming back.' Tears of relief welled up in her eyes.

'Well, I very nearly didn't make it, lassie. My wee boat and I have come through one hell of a battering. I'd hoped you'd find this old place to shelter. It used to be the nurse's house years ago.'

Jess burst into tears. Sandy put a comforting arm around her shoulder.

'What on earth's the matter, lassie? You look like you've seen a ghost.'

The mention of ghosts made her weep all the more.

'Here lassie, have a wee nip of this.' He handed her a pewter whisky flask. 'Go on. It'll help calm you down.'

She took a sip of the golden liquid. The whisky burned her throat as it slipped down, instantly imparting its warming effect on her shivering body.

'Thanks, that's warmed me up a bit,' she said handing the flask back. Through her tear-stained face she forced a wan smile.

Sandy listened intently as she told him about how she'd twisted her ankle and then taken shelter in the kirk and cottage. He stroked the bristles on his chin thoughtfully. 'There's something you're not telling me lassie. Something's scared you, hasn't it? Something's put the fear of God into you!'

Wiping her eyes with her handkerchief, Jess tried to pull herself together.

'There was a woman in this house.' Her heart sank at the expression of puzzlement on his face.

'A woman, you say? But, lassie, there hasn't been anyone living on the island since 1962. Well apart from the lighthouse keeper and his family, who left in 1997 when the lighthouse was automated.'

'But, I saw a woman as clearly as I'm seeing you. She was sitting in this very chair. When I went closer to her she disappeared. I've heard a child crying, too.'

He sat silently for a moment deep in thought. 'This woman, what did she look like?'

'She was young and slim with grey sorrowful eyes. She wore a black dress and a dark blue shawl around her shoulders.'

'Did she speak at all?' he asked.

'No, she said nothing, but looked so pitifully sad.'

Sandy sighed, pulling the whisky flask out of his coat pocket. He took a long swig before offering it to her. She declined.

'Well, there's one thing for sure lass; we're not going to get off the island until morning. Hopefully by then the storm will have passed and it'll be safe to cross the Firth. We'll just have to sit out the storm here.'

'Sandy, do you believe in ghosts?'

He took a moment before answering. 'Well, I've never seen one, but I've met plenty who reckon they have. Let's just say, I keep an open mind. I've lived in Caithness all of my life and over the years I've heard many stories about Stroma. Many believe that the ghosts of deceased islanders still haunt the island. There are local books in Thurso library. Maybe there's one about Stroma, you never know.'

'These people who say they've seen ghosts, could I meet them?'

'It might be better to leave well alone lass.'

She said nothing as she stared at the door, half expecting the ghostly woman to appear at any moment.

'We'll rest here until it gets light and then see what state the sea is in. Hopefully we'll have you back across the water by lunchtime. We need to get that ankle of yours looked at too. How's it feeling?'

Getting up from the chair she tried to put her weight on it. An excruciating pain shot up her leg, making her fall back into the chair.

'Not so good, obviously. Don't worry lass, we'll find some way of getting you back to the boat.'

The rest of the night passed with both of them sleeping a while and talking about ghosts and the supernatural.

Shafts of sun streamed through the grimy windows as Jess emerged from a fretful slumber. Momentarily forgetting that she'd a twisted ankle, she tried to get out of her chair. Her scream of pain woke Sandy with a jolt.

'Hey, steady on, lass, you stay put.' Hauling himself upright, he ambled over to the window and looked outside. 'The weather gods are smiling on us, lass.'

It took a mere twenty minutes for the *Song of the Sea* to make the short voyage across the now becalmed Pentland Firth. Once ashore, Sandy drove Jess straight to the local surgery, where the doctor strapped up her twisted ankle. With Jess's medical needs dealt with, Sandy picked up her beloved motorcycle from Gills Bay delivering her and the bike to her home in Reay.

'Right now lass, don't forget our wee arrangement. You owe me a painting of Stroma.' He scribbled his telephone number on a scrap of paper and handed it to her. 'Just give me a ring when you're up to it lass and we can discuss which view of Stroma to paint.'

With the Stroma photographs downloaded to her computer's hard drive, she started to browse through them. The first few images were rather unremarkable. Suddenly her heart missed a beat, the hairs on the back of her neck stood erect. The photograph was the first one she'd taken at The Gloup. A faint image of a woman wearing a black dress and blue shawl was standing on the edge of the deep chasm. In her arms, she held a small child.

Jess quickly moved onto the next shot, convinced that when she returned to it, the ghostly apparition would be gone. An icy shudder travelled down her spine when she saw the ghostly figures were still there. They appeared semi-translucent, as if superimposed onto the photograph.

She'd give Sandy a ring and let him look at them.

Jess brought her motorbike to a halt at the end of the road. Sandy's instructions had been clear enough.

He lived in a croft about half a mile down the road that terminated at the lighthouse.

'So you found me okay then, lass, come in and I'll get the kettle on.'

She followed him into a small living room and sank down into a brown well-worn leather sofa. There were books lying on every flat surface, including the floor.

Sandy shuffled into the room with two mugs of tea and a bag of sugar. 'There's sugar here if you want it, lass.' He handed one of the mugs to her. 'So you got some good photos did you, lass?'

'They're interesting let's put it that way. There's one in particular I want you to see.'

Jess scrolled through the first few, with Sandy making polite comments about each. As the image appeared on the screen, Sandy stared at the eerie figures standing on the edge of the Gloup. Jess watched his face intently, trying to read it.

'So who are these two, Sandy? They weren't there when I took the photo.'

He suddenly looked melancholy, as if he was about to cry. 'Poor lassie and her wee bairn, they didn't deserve to die. I've seen them from time to time, when I've been alone on the island.'

Frowning, Jess looked him straight in the eye. 'I thought you told me you'd never seen a ghost.'

He looked at her, defeated. 'I'm sorry lass, I didn't want to scare you.'

'So, who are they?'

'She was a nurse and the child was her three year old daughter. Her husband discovered that he was not the child's father and in a drunken rage flung them both over the cliff edge onto the rocks below. The woman roams the island desperately looking for her child. It's said that they're only ever seen together at the Gloup. I guess it's because that's where they both died. The father was hanged for the crime.'

'But who were they?' Jess repeated.

'As far as I recall the lassie was called Mary and her wee bairn Jessica. Aye that's right, Mary and Jessica Palmer.

A poem for Jessie Ivy Macleod

Meg Macleod

night-nurse

I watch the moon
I follow the frost
defining and articulating
cold upon the window pane

I have become an ocean of heartbeats
rising and falling
a point of focus
for one who cannot yet see with clarity

for one who listens
lying against the sea-rhythm of my heart
and is comforted through the long night
while her mother sleeps towards healing

Wednesdays at the Oak Cask

Sharon Gunason Pottinger

Carol on Carol

My name says it all. Carol. Carol means song and that's me. I love singin'. All kinds. I go to three churches because the music – some of it anyhoo – is so beautiful. I mean it gives you the shivers. In a nice way. I sing with the choir and I think it's like being with angels. Oh I know some devils in there, too, they'll cut your throat for a solo. Not me. I get my time in front as a chanteuse – that's French for a high class singer – every Wednesday. Beatles music. Everyone loves the Beatles, right? Not like I'm stuck on the 70's or anything like that. It's popular with the audience at the Oak Cask and you gotta give folks what they want. Once a week and three times on a Sunday is not enough to pay the bills, so I have my day job – nails. My best friend is a dental hygienist. She makes a lot more money 'n me but I couldn't stand my hands in people's mouths all day. Yuk. She tells me that hands are dirtier than people's mouths, but I get to put their hands right away into washing liquid I tell her. She says she is in the health care profession and I'm just a nail technician. I let her have that last word cuz she's my best friend and I feel like she needs that assurance. I don't need that because I know I am on my way to someplace else. I'm saving up money staying at home with Mum. She likes the company and I dinna mind her really. She gives some talk now and then about coming in all hours of the night and the money I spend on what she calls la-di-dah no going to church in them clothes, but I remind her that I am a chanteuse and the dresses are all part of it. I ask her did she ever see Cilla Black wearing go to church clothes when she was singin'? She harumphs without ever givin' in, but I know she loves me. Sometimes on a Saturday night if I don't have a gig, I'll dress up and put on backing tapes and sing all night to me mum. We wind up the two of us singing and crying when we do 'Over the Rainbow'.

Jimmy on Jimmy

I'm nae bad lookin'. Not like elephant man. But not a heart stopper either. My face wouldna scare wee bairns, but I'll never be a poster on some lassie's wall. I'm a drummer. I'm used to being in the back providing the rhythm that keeps others going. I'm used to seeing the backs of people getting all the attention. I dinna mind that because I love my drums. When I have my sticks in my hand, I feel alive. Like nothing can be better. Until I get a keek o' Carol. She sings up front. That's where she should be if you ask me. She is sleek like a salmon in her chanteuse dresses and her eyes are deep and soft. It makes me feel like I'm meltin' so it does. Once I even forgot my drummin' when she looked at me while singing 'And I love him'. I picked it up right on the beat, so the audience, if they were nae too drunk to notice, took it for a 'dramatic pause' – that's what Carol called it when I went to tell her 'Sorry.' Every Wednesday we play at The Oak Cask. I live for Wednesdays.

Wednesday at the Oak Cask

Jimmy smiles as he reads the blackboard out front:

Get your ticket to ride on the New Yellow Submarine
Live Music tonight
Free

Not quite the bright lights, but a gig is a gig. The Oak Cask is 'making an asset out of a deficit' – so the proposal to the enterprise bunch said when they granted the funding for refurbing the old train station as a pub. He goes around to the back to make sure the sign is there on the trackside as well. Not that many people stop, but that was how Gordon found them, riding the trains with that pal of his who goes all around Scotland by train just so he can tick off the places he's been. Gordon takes the train up from Glasgow when his friend is away on the rigs. Jimmy has always believed that someday he'd take that same train down the road to the bigger things the city offers musicians.

Once he's checked the perimeter, Jimmy moves to the raised platform that acts as stage to set up the cables and amps. A new waitress brings him his pint. Looking up at him on the stage, she blurts out, 'Those are the smallest feet I've ever seen.'

'Small feet, big heart, Darlin,' Jimmy responds and turns back to the equipment on the little stage. He knows all too well that the two waitresses will be tittering about men and the size of their feet. He loved his Italian grandmother, but the legacy from that tiny touch of the Mediterranean in his blood is not just his little feet. He has a dark beard – had to shave twice a day when he was still in school. He used to think he'd grow into some kind of Italian lover, but that was just it – he didn't grow. He busied himself with setting up. If he gets done before Carol arrives, there's time for some conversation. And tonight he has something exciting to share with her. An appointment for a session in a recording studio. Just a session drummer, but the beginning of something steady.

'Oh, here he is now, the man of the hour,' Eilidh, the manager, says from behind the bar as the new girl turns around to see a tall, broad, dark-haired man loping into the pub. 'Gordon, this is the new girl, Catriona.'

Gordon takes her hand in his giant hand, surprisingly soft, and kisses it.

'OK, Lancelot'. Eilidh says, 'Make yourself useful. Take yer pint and another one for Jimmy over to the stage.'

Gordon bows, and moves carefully with the two pints toward the stage.

'Is Carol here yet, Jimmy?' Gordon asks, putting down Jimmy's new pint.

Jimmy tenses. Gordon is literally twice the man he is. He likes the man, but always feels small next to him. Gordon's mention of Carol set his teeth on edge.

Carol walks in with a garment bag over her arm and giant rollers in her hair. She smiles and waves at the boys, nods to Eilidh, and picks up a Diet Coke at the bar, heading for her dressing room. Jimmy watches her fondly. Seeing Carol *before* she becomes diva has the kind of intimacy Jimmy imagines they might have over breakfast in their own kitchen someday.

'I wonder what she's wearing tonight?' Gordon says to no one in particular. 'I love to watch the way she moves in those long dresses of hers.'

Gordon is one of a very few devoted followers of the New Yellow Submarine, so Jimmy holds his tongue, but he can't help clenching his fists hard. Someday he and Gordon will have it out. Jimmy doesn't care how big the guy is.

It wasn't until their break that Jimmy had a chance to tell Carol about the agent that left his card. *I know we hear that kind of stuff a lot. He said they need a drummer for session work. Not much money for the session, but you get royalties.* I didn't take too much notice of it, but I called the number and I have an appointment.

Carol reached across the table and took Jimmy's hands in hers, 'I'm so glad for you!'

Jimmy almost forgot the most important part of his speech, which he had so carefully rehearsed, 'And I thought when I got back, you and I might go out to celebrate.'

Gordon could feel Jimmy's nerves unravelling as he watched the two of them. He had been so busy watching Carol that he had not sussed Jimmy's struggle between love and nerves.

'That would be great! Let's do it.'

Gordon wondered if Jimmy and Carol had the same idea about what it meant to celebrate.

Next Wednesday, Gordon arrived to a very different atmosphere in the Oak Cask. The waitresses were silent and Jimmy was setting up with an unusual stiffness about his moves.

'Jimmy, what's wrong?'

'I didn't get the gig.' Jimmy blurted out. 'What can I say to Carol. I can't lie, but I have no big news, nothing to offer her.'

'I have an idea. I've been wanting to tell you both something for a while. You'd be helping me out, too.' Before Gordon could explain, the guitarists started playing the intro and Jimmy rose to take his place on the stage. Jimmy looked more sad eyed than Malcolm thought possible.

'Just trust me, Jimmy, OK? Follow my lead?' Gordon stage whispered to Jimmy as he climbed to the stage as if it were the gallows. Jimmy radiated misery almost all the way to his fingertips, but his drumming was all he had and he put himself into it each time, every time. Gordon admired him even more than he had after watching him all these weeks and decided he had to rescue his friends.

Friday at the Copa

> *Tonight's stars include*
> *Trudy Garland*
> *Bella Fitzgerald*
> *and the precision dancing of the Copa choristers*

'I'm so glad you wanted to include me in your celebration, thanks, Jimmy,' Carol said.

'It was Gordon's idea. He really wanted us both to be here.'
Carol laughed. 'I've never worn this dress except on stage or at home singing to my mum.'

'You look...' Jimmy stopped like a car stuck between gears.

Carol tilted her head and waited.

'Beautiful. I don't have good words…'

'Beautiful will do nicely,' and she hugged him. 'Come to think of it, I've never seen you in a suit before.'

'Gordon helped me pick it out.'

'He's been so nervous about this all. He stopped by yesterday and I helped him get ready and soothed his nerves -- that seemed even more important than getting his nails right.'

'He came to see you?' Jimmy was struggling to keep his jealousy in check. He knew it was stupid. Here he was with Carol, and Gordon had made it possible. He should be grateful. And then, 'You did his nails?'

'Yes. Said he was much too nervous to do it right, and the Ruby Red colour would show up any glitches.'

'Oh, I see,' said Jimmy, baffled. Then Carol slipped her arm through his and there was no room in his brain for thinking anything other than how wonderful it was to be arm in arm with her, breathing in her scent, seeing the sparkle of an earring, a tiny wisp of hair curling out of line with the others in front of her ear. The thought of running his finger through her hair – just to tuck it back into place preoccupied him completely as the curtain went up.

The Copa choristers filled the little stage to overflowing with their costumes of giant feathered headdresses and shiny, skimpy dresses with elaborate bows and flourishes. The dancing was precise if not as elaborate as the costumes. And then there was a drum roll – not a particularly good one, Jimmy couldn't help noticing, and Trudy Garland, the night's star, appeared. Jimmy had never seen such a large woman, and she didn't seem to look much like Judy Garland, but Carol was delighted, applauding uproariously. 'Doesn't Gordon look great? I would never have imagined…'

Jimmy did a double take and managed to mutter only, 'I wouldn't have imagined it either in a million years.'

After champagne and flowers in Trudy Garland's dressing room, the three of them went back to Gordon's flat for more champagne. Gordon and Carol talked and laughed about panty girdles and how to repair tights that so quickly go laddery while Jimmy drank and watched them. In that curious insightfulness that comes with the bubbles in champagne just before falling asleep and forgetting it all, Jimmy noted Gordon's Ruby Red nails as he poured out the last of the champagne. 'Thas a bootiful job on your nails, Gordon. Really like the colour. Is it OK to say you make a fine figger of a woman?'

Gordon smiled, and looking down at his nails, overbalanced and fell heavily on the end of the sofa, narrowly avoiding Jimmy's feet. 'Och, Jimmy, I love your drummin', man, but I am so jealous of your feet!'

'Ma feet, wha the fuck? Oh 'scuse me Carol. So sorry.'

Carol, sitting on the floor of Gordon's small sitting room singing one of Sunday's choral songs softly to herself, said, 'No worries, Jimmy. I've heard the word before. No need to treat me like a china doll.'

'Yeah, Jimmy, your feet,' Gordon said, raising his own bare foot up closer to eye level, 'can you imagine how hard it is to find heels in a size 11?'

'Never thought about that I must confesh,' Jimmy said as the bubbles took hold of his brain.

The Sapling

Meg Macleod

The young sapling stands out against the skyline. The bare grass and rocks around it are skirted by heather. Beyond the skyline, slightly south-west, rise the shoulders of Ben Hope. Morag's path, a thin thread of grey ground, begins at the cottage and ends here at the tiny Rowan. From here she looks south towards a different country of which she knows nothing.

'Do you think we might travel abroad this year?

James gives the reply she expects. 'What on earth for? And how can we with the work on the croft? And besides, we can't afford it.'

His mind returns to the matters in hand; a tractor broken down, a fence to be mended, not to mention the upkeep on the boat. None of these things are a 'problem' to James. They are the lifeblood of his existence, filling his mind with creative challenges, tiring his body into blissful sleep at the end of the day. Morag completes the pattern of his days. He is not looking for anything else in the self-contained village cut off from the world by fourteen miles of almost impassable road around the Kyle, and the Kyle itself running out the length of the village to the open sea completing the illusion of isolation.

'I've never been past Tongue,' she says. 'There's talk of building a causeway. That will make it easier to travel.'

'There's nothing south, just hills. Being pregnant is making you mithery.' He gives her a swift peck on the cheek, grins and

114

departs. 'Don't forget to do those forms for the grazing's officer.'

'I won't.' She turns to look out at the hill behind the house feeling an empathy with the sapling tree already bending to the will of the wind, and settling into its particular peculiar lopsided shape. She places her hand on her belly where the baby is kicking.

She finishes the forms, puts them ready for the postie to collect.

The chickens make a dive for her when she appears, thinking she has food for them and make complaining squawks at her when they see she is empty handed. They spread out, back-stepping and scratching their way through the damp, rough terrain. She pushes through deep heather out onto the close-cropped hilltop. She sits down beside the tree. To the north is only the ocean, islands close to shore, a harbour with small boats at anchor. She looks down across the houses that edge the road going through the village. She knows them all, yet she knows no-one with whom she can share the peculiar dissatisfaction she feels; a restlessness to be away, to travel, to find out what lies south of the mountains.

Daniel is born in springtime. Her life is suddenly filled with more work than she can imagine. For the first few weeks, while he is tiny, she carries him strapped to her, Indian style. Her head is full of the possibilities for her son as she works on the croft.

She takes him every day to the tree and tells stories about the land beyond the mountain as she imagines it.

A sea-change occurs almost as soon as he can walk. His father begins to take him along to the croft, to learn. 'Can't start them too young,' he says to Morag proudly. Queenie, the collie, one of a long line of Queenies, walks alongside as if she knows he will be master one day. Morag watches them, reluctantly giving up her child to James' practical and demanding world.

Morag has other plans for her boy. She has her eyes on the south for him.

115

At five years old Daniel is strong and determined, perfectly capable of surviving the rough and tumble of falling off walls and scraping his knees and being in charge of Queenie. His affinity with animals manifests itself in the wee mice he carries in his pockets and the tadpoles he fusses over in the pond. He is often found asleep beside the lambs in the byre.

The sapling tree is no longer a thin and spindly accident upon the hill. It has grown strong. Its main branch leaning outwards, pointing south like an arrow on the skyline. It`s just tall enough to sit beneath. '

Look Daniel. The tree is pointing south.'

'What`s south.'

'Oh, so many things, warmth, adventures, its where the swallows go in winter you know, the ones that nest in the byre every year. The tree shows them the way.'

'Why is there only one tree?'

She continues to plant the seeds of imagination into Daniel. 'I don't know, maybe a Robin planted it, to be a sign post.' An imaginary white lie will not hurt, she thinks.

'Can I go south with the swallows?'

'One day when you are older.'

Daniel begins to talk to the robin, also the blackbirds, and the gulls. He begins to draw pictures of them.

The distance between herself and her husband widens as the closed reality of the croft begins to encircle the child. Daniel prefers to draw rather than work with his father on the land. And because Morag understands Daniel, she defends his defiance. It causes a rift between herself and James. The rift widens and begins to come between Daniel and his father. It consolidates as the years pass; turbulent years; the two people around whom her world turns see life from different perspectives.

Morag, intervening in an argument, tries to align James to her thinking, 'The boy has real talent, he should be encouraged. My father had the same talent. It died with him...all those unrealised dreams.'

116

Morag grows strong in her belief in Daniel. She withstands the anger from James, turning her back to him as the sapling turns away from the biting wind. She no longer forms part of his pattern and the nights grow cold for them both. The jigsaw of their lives scatters across the years. Yet she clings to her opinion and to the defence of her son. He is a life-raft on which her dreams drift on an unknown current.

'I'm going south, Mam,' he says one day.

Morag's heart flutters with a combination of pain and hope. She had dreamed this for him and yet, without him, what will she do?

'The school sent away a portfolio of my work. I have an interview at the art college. They said it was exceptional. I can start...'

Hearing the conversation, James interrupts.

'What about the croft?'

Daniel shakes his head.

Morag watches Daniel leave on the post bus.

James walks away from Morag. 'Now look what you have done.' He throws the words over his shoulder at her.

Morag walks to the Rowan tree and weeps.

The National Geographic send Daniel on safari to Africa to study and draw the birds and animals. His own book is published with detailed observations and diary entries of the many countries that he visits. There is a dedication inside which reads, 'for my mother and the tree, both which pointed south.'

He gives it to them on a visit home between assignments.

James reads the inscription in the book but lays it aside without reading further, only acknowledging, grudgingly that Daniel 'is doing quite well' if anyone should ask him 'How is Daniel?'

James cannot forgive Morag for the loss of his son to the outside world or for the dedication in the book. His thinking does not go beyond the slow walks he took with Daniel holding his hand tightly, proudly pointing out the lay of the land and the small acres of croft that would one day be his.

On the kitchen wall there are postcards from many different countries

Daniel is careful about what he writes on his postcards. He omits to tell his mother of the hardships and poverty that he finds in so many of the places through which his work takes him. He preserves her innocence of the world south of the mountains. A few white lies won't hurt he thinks, remembering the stories she told him in her effort to create the world she herself had failed to find.

Morag takes the postcards with her to the tree, reading them and looking out towards the mountains.

`He hopes to be home this year, 1969, perhaps...`, Morag reads a letter out loud to James.

`He hopes to make it next year, 1970, well, if everything goes to plan.` A postcard informs them of his change of direction.

Morag writes back to him. *They are building a causeway. Daniel, will you manage home this year? 1972. It's been a long, long time.*

His last letter tells Morag that he is doing conservation work with the RSPB.

The tree on the hill has taken a beating from storms of winter. Its main branch lies broken. So deeply is she connected to the tree that she sees this as a prophesy.

'I think Daniel will be home this year,' she says to James.

'Not before time.'

The south is beginning to creep up and over the causeway. Visitors come bringing their different accents and opinions. Morag and James draw closer together in the comfort of familiarity and find new patterns in which to survive, each of them recognizing the strength in the outline of the life they have together. James is getter tired. It's hard for him to keep up with the work. A new incentive brings salvation.

Morag writes to tell Daniel of the change in their fortune:

Daniel, exciting news, your father is getting paid to do nothing, well not nothing, but wait till I tell you, it's to do with Corncrakes, trying to get them back onto the crofts, so your dad agreed to let his croft be a pilot scheme. Who would have thought it? Corncrakes, can't stand the sound of them, but it won't matter, I don't hear too well lately. It would be nice to see you, soon, I hope, love Mam.

A letter by return post arrives.

Dear Mam,
I will be home this springtime for certain. Perhaps you better sit down. I am the person in charge of the Corncrake project. I didn't want to tell you till it was all organised. I've missed home. Can't wait to walk up to the tree with you. Tell Dad I will be able to help out on the croft. You don't need to tell him any more than that. I will enjoy telling him myself.

Dear Daniel,
That is good news and what a surprise. Can't believe you never told us.
The tree has lost its arm, but it's still standing. You know it was me that planted it. It wasn't a robin. It was a sapling uprooted while your dad was clearing a space for the field shelter. It seemed wrong to let it die, it being a Rowan. I dug it in deep to give it shelter expecting something magical to happen. It seemed a lovely thing to have to dream upon. I guess my dreams went astray and landed on you. Your Dad is pleased and surprised that you're coming home to help out,
love mam.

Daniel finds her sitting beneath the tree, its bark rough and worn, its limbs sparse and broken. The early summer sun is rising from the south east casting a rosy glow. For a few precious minutes both the tree and his mother appear young again.

He stands looking south over the mountains of his childhood towards the years spent away from his home. Overhead, far away in the sky a pattern of geese is circling. He closes his eyes to listen to them.

His mother watches him and waits for him to tell his story.

Call from the Sea

Tricia Knight

It began as just a normal day. I unpacked in the afternoon and called Mum and Dad from the telephone box in Main Street, Castletown, in the North of Scotland, to let them know I'd arrived safely. I felt a creeping heaviness in my eyelids, which wasn't surprising – we'd driven over six hundred miles from our flat in Leighton Buzzard. Since acquiring the cottage for our eventual retirement, I'd only spent one week in it.

I was looking forward to my October break and beginning the refurbishment. The first time I walked through the front door, I was bathed in the peaceful atmosphere. It was going to be my sanctuary from all the woes that ate at me running the hostel back home in Leighton Buzzard.

I was happy as I flicked the lamp on and pushed out the remnants of the day. Settled in my comfy, mottled armchair and listening to my Grieg CD, I was looking forward to toasting my frozen toes by a crackling coal fire until bed time. After about ten minutes, my blissful evening was interrupted by a loud knock on the front door.

My elderly neighbour Kitty, stood in the dim porch in front of a policeman. Both wore serious expressions.

My heart leapt. 'What's happened?' I asked.

The constable removed his hat and asked me to confirm my name. Once I had, he informed me that my father had collapsed and died at three o'clock, just two hours earlier.

I had delayed installing a telephone when we'd signed the mortgage, hoping to use its absence to enjoy a little peace and rare privacy for a couple of months.

I reasoned that I was only here for a week at a time at present, and intended having it installed before we moved up permanently. I never dreamt my dad might die so suddenly. To say I felt selfish and guilty was an understatement. I was devastated.

I hadn't heard of this place until my new partner, Hamish, suggested I visit the area. He wanted to know if I could live here. Hamish had originated from the far North, Thurso to be exact, and he'd always ached to return to his roots.

Once I arrived in the town, I understood why he wanted me to experience the place before making my decision. It was vastly different from middle England. Many folk would struggle with its remoteness, lack of trees, lack of shops and the bustle available in the South.

I was intrigued, in love and so overworked that I was a prime candidate for a quieter, slower pace of life. As I explored the area I was conscious of the vast curve of Dunnet Bay beckoning me towards its windswept dunes and huge breakers. I also noticed a two bedroomed cottage for sale at the edge of the village of Castletown as I passed through.

Captivated, I quickly agreed to move north with Hamish. We could purchase that cottage and find employment.

Mum recoiled in horror when I told her where we were moving to. Understandably I thought. It was a long way away. My children, all adults, were fine about me relocating, even planning to land on us for holidays. A real shock was how my father had reacted immediately I mentioned the move. My quietly spoken dad erupted, crimson faced, into a hissy fit. I assumed that, like mother, he would miss me. I was soon to discover I was mistaken about the reasons for their objections.

Still shocked, the morning after the terrible news, I wandered to the shore just after sunrise. Apart from an icy blast assailing my ears and gulls screeching overhead, the three-mile-long beach was deserted. I prayed aloud, earnestly.

'Dad, I'm so sorry. I love you. If you know how, show me you're aware, somehow. Send me a sign.' I listened and searched the misty horizon.

Apart from a fleeting sensation of something wrapping around my shoulders and a fragrance similar to my deceased Nanna's talc wafting around my face, I received nothing. I was incredibly disappointed that he hadn't come through.

I'd grown up experiencing apparitions, disembodied faces and premonitions, so I expected to hear from Dad. Mind, he had dismissed all that as imaginary gobbledegook.

Only my Nanna Alice had listened and when I turned twelve, she took me to her home in Barnet, London, for the summer holidays. While I was there she took me to her church for the first time. I didn't know what to expect, but I knew mum disapproved of Nanna's religion.

There were no icons, just a stage with dusky pink curtains and a lectern, surrounded by multi-coloured floral displays. The hall had huge Georgian windows, through which filtered long shafts of sunlight. The people talked among themselves and there was an air of expectancy before the speaker took her place by the Lectern. I heard prayers said for the sick as their names were read from a book and various accounts were given of healing. It was very spiritual and some of the speakers told of similar experiences to mine. I looked at Nanna and she smiled.

'Has that answered some of your questions?' she asked me at the end of the service.

'I think it has, Nanna, but what kind of church is it?'

She explained that it was a Christian Science Church. Followers believed they could receive healing through the prayers of others and that signs and other information were communicated from heaven. The church aimed to ease the suffering of those who were sick, or bereaved.

I was raised as Church of England so found the CSC very different, but I felt we were kindred spirits and it explained my visitations sensibly. I never felt I was odd, afraid or confused after that, although I didn't share my experiences with anyone else until I met Hamish.

A week after dad's funeral in November, Mum dropped a bombshell.
'Dad never wanted me to tell you, but I think you have a right to know...you were someone else's child. Dad met me after I'd been abandoned and agreed to raise you as his own.'

As if to justify the lies they'd raised me on, she added hesitantly, 'Do you see? He loved you and me enough to do that.' Her voice trailed away and she bit her lip as she searched my face waiting for my reaction.

Dumfounded, I must have resembled a fish out of water as I stood there gasping, trying to make sense of her disclosure. I felt cheated, betrayed and physically sick. Shaken to the core, I found it difficult to formulate the questions I needed answers to.

'Why didn't you tell me, Mum? I can understand why not when I was little, but surely you should have told me when I grew up.'

'There was never a right time, and besides no-one else knows. I could have kept quiet, I probably should have. He was someone I met briefly when I was in the WAAF in Castletown during the war. That's why, when you said you were moving there, dad got upset. You were his daughter and he didn't want to lose you.'

A mixture of anger and fear rose in my throat,

'Who am I then, who is my other father?' I choked and swallowed hard. When I look back now, I wish I had shown more compassion and gratitude to her, but I felt too raw in the moment.

Mum, paled. 'He...was a Canadian airman, or so he told me. We saw each other just three times. To my shame, long enough for me to fall for him. Then he disappeared. I did ask the officer in charge of the squadron for an address, but he said he wasn't allowed to divulge confidential information to anyone other than relatives of personnel.

'There were three pilots, known as *The Musketeers*, and we went out in a group on our last date. One of them married a local girl, who I had a lot in common with. We got on well and the day your father disappeared I went to her hoping she could ask her chap where he'd gone. She was sitting in the canteen sobbing her heart out. Her husband had just been killed during a training flight.

'Before I could look any further, I was re-posted, with my battered pride, to Bedford. The rest, my girl, is history. Just don't... ask me anymore now.'

She was exhausted. I'd kept on at her too long, to my eternal shame.

'Soon I'll look for a photograph I had, but it'll do you no good,' she said. Then Mum broke down and I knew she wouldn't be drawn further.

Poor Mum, she had just lost Dad, and I realise with hindsight, she was very brave to tell me the truth at such a time. I'm convinced now she thought she was going to join dad soon and wanted to tidy things up before she did.

Sure enough, Mum's funeral took place the same month. We cleared the house and visited the solicitor. Once my parents' estate was settled, I took all the old photos and a few keepsakes, and Hamish and I moved up to Caithness. We found work with different housing associations, and our neighbours were so welcoming that we decided to volunteer to give something back to the village in our spare time. I signed up with the local heritage centre and helped catalogue old photographs and memorabilia as they were donated. It was great fun, tracing people's history, finding out how they spent their days in years gone by. I thought I might discover more about my biological father's identity during my research.

We'd only been living here a week when I was awakened by a loud droning noise. The house vibrated as an aircraft passed overhead. It seemed to go on and on. I'd never heard a plane so

125

low before. I wondered if there was going to be a crash and, alarmed, I shot out of bed. Then it stopped. I lay down again, strained my ears and eventually dozed off. With Hamish working away, there had been no-one else in the house for me to ask whether there had been a noise. The following day I quizzed my neighbours, but they hadn't heard anything. I couldn't verify whether I'd really heard a plane or I'd dreamt it.

Over the next couple of days, I wondered if some spirit was trying to communicate and direct me towards my father's identity.

I did my turn that Sunday at the centre and we were told there was going to be an exhibition about the role of the Airfield at Castletown during World War Two. It seemed such a co-incidence.

When I got home, full of anticipation, I grabbed the oldest photo album and checked it. There was nothing unusual inside, just pictures and postcards of mum and dad in and following the war. When I'd had enough of searching, all I had to show for it was a mammoth headache. I leaned over to put the book back and in my clumsiness I knocked the other album off the table. It split the binding and a pocket fell out, spilling cards and letters. To my surprise there was a faded, black and white photograph of my Mum and another woman with two airmen. I turned it over and read some words penned in faint blue ink:

Lots of love, Joy, from Maurice xx

It had to be him. Joy was my mother's name.

Well wrapped up against the blustering wind, I locked up and strode down to the bay. The tide was rushing in, battering the shore with emerald foaming breakers. The harsh north wind bit my face and stung my ears. The dark clouds were mountainous, threatening a deluge of hail or snow. But none of that mattered. I calmed myself, gave thanks and begged to be heard. I prayed for clarification, wanting to know if the signs I had received were intended.

The cold intensified, biting at my fingers and toes through my gloves and boots. I shrank deeper under the scarf encasing my neck and waited. I stamped about in the moving sea of sand for half an hour, with no response. I moved to leave, accepting that I wasn't going to receive anything. The wind still howled and the bitterly sharp spray seemed to chase me away. Crossing some slime-covered flagstones, I stumbled, fell and banged my shin. I saw stars and heard a plane sweeping down from the sky. A second later, it stopped and my senses returned. I glanced around embarrassed, hoping no-one saw me fall.

Luckily, I couldn't see anyone. Cursing my clumsiness, I made my way up the rocky bank to the car park. By then my knee was aching and bleeding quite badly and my coat was dirty. I just wanted to get home.

I'd begun my trek up the hill, when a man pulled up in his van. Keeping the engine running, he shouted across. 'Can I give you a lift? You look like you've had a fall and I think I know where you live. I'm going your way, so it's no trouble.'

For once, I was willing to accept a lift from a stranger and gladly climbed in. The cold, and my wet shoes made me shiver, but home was only a quarter of a mile up the road. I just had time to thank him when we arrived at the front of my house. As I got out, he smiled and wished me well. His eyes twinkled and it was only as I waved him off that I realised he looked familiar. I hadn't even asked his name. The only thing I knew about him was his van's number plate and that he lived nearby.

I rushed in and ran a hot bath. While I was soaking in the lavender suds, it hit me. *His moustache, that smile, in fact his whole face was the image of the man in Mum's photo. The van's number plate was ironic too, M43 RAF.*

I sat up so fast that soapsuds splashed into my eyes, making them smart.

Thank you, Musketeer. For bringing me a sign, thank you. I dressed quickly, wanting to search the internet. I started with Caithness.org and World War Two, for any lists of airmen stationed here in nineteen forty three, but I couldn't find one. A little disheartened, I gave up.

The next couple of days were uneventful, until I was driving home across the Causewaymire. I heard the rumbling noise of a heavy aircraft, and then a hundred yards in front of me, a dark green wartime plane cruised slowly across the road about a hundred feet in the air. It quickly became obscured by the sunset, leaving me stunned. I was certain then, some-one was trying to lead me to something.

When I arrived for my next shift at the centre, I found old George in the office, nearly buried beneath boxes of photographs and maps.

'You'll like this, Eileen.' He beamed up at me. 'We're having a World War Two themed exhibition this month.'

He'd seen my photograph, but being a fairly recent incomer like myself, hadn't known many people or the history of the area at that time either. '

'Just stick your picture up here on the white board with a card underneath it. Other untitled letters, cards and pictures will be here and, as visitors recognise people and places, they'll add their information and memories.'

His words raised my hopes and, as the exhibition ran, the footfall was high. Connections were found between contributions and signified by using lines of green string. I studied the board with interest each time I was on shift, always disappointed to find that my little photograph remained an island.

Towards the end of the last week, George called me and said they had received a letter for me. Within a few minutes I covered the mile to the centre. I practically tore the envelope open and a card with a photograph similar to the one I had, fell out. But this group had an extra airman in it and the business card had a telephone number with Mr Iain McLennan written on it.

Buzzing at the prospect of finally resolving the mystery, I was lifting my coat off the stand when a new pamphlet caught my eye. It had a slogan about the war and an aerial photograph of the village. Intrigued, I started reading. It contained witness statements of incidents that had taken place between 1939 and the end of the War.

One testimonial in particular aroused my curiosity. A man described how he'd been watching spitfires training over the bay. Unfortunately, the lead plane misjudged his manoeuvre and smashed into the sea. There were few details, except that the pilot and his plane were never recovered.

Was that the pull of the bay? Could my father be there?

I walked to Olrig Cemetery to study the war graves of airmen killed while at the airfield, but there was no Maurice there.

I rechecked the Caithness.org history of World War 2 information and found a link to another military history site. It gave details of all crashes and airmen killed throughout the war. I made very slow progress, but eventually found three air crashes in our part of Caithness. One was a Maurice Chevalier, killed in a spitfire training sortie over the bay.

Was that my Maurice?

Determined to find out, I rang Mr McLennan hoping he would be able to throw more light in my direction. He told me his mother was the other woman in my snapshot and thought she might be able to help me. She was in a care home.

I visited the next day with Iain McLennan. He introduced me to his mother, Joy. I was surprised. Joy was also my mother's name.

My head felt light as she filled in some of the gaping holes in my history.

She smiled as she recalled the three inseparable air men labelled playfully by my mum and her as *The Musketeers*. Joy had married one of them. Her photograph was taken just after her marriage to Maurice and my mother, a witness, had been sent a similar one as a keepsake.

Maurice was Iain's step-father. Maurice was the handsome black-haired man pictured sporting a 'spiv' moustache. So

Maurice *wasn't* my father. The other two just disappeared around the same time as Maurice died. Mrs MacLennan seemed a bit confused as to which one was involved with my mother, but at least she told me their names. One was Angus something and the other was Greg Merrick.

She said she'd heard later from the one called Angus. While clearing Maurice's locker, Angus found signed photographs of the wedding. He'd sent her pictures with a brief note to say that he was being re-posted and would get in touch after the war. He never did.

I updated George when he asked me about my visit. He said he'd put an appeal on the Canadian Veterans forum and checked air crash listings on the web.

My head was spinning with it all. I felt I was tantalisingly close. I visited the bay and thanked Maurice, because I was certain it was his spirit trying to help me.

It was time for the War Exhibition to be taken down, and we'd just finished packing and labelling it all when the phone rang.

George answered it and nodded. 'I'll tell her. I'm sorry for your loss, Iain.' George replaced the receiver and announced that Mrs McLennan had passed away peacefully in her sleep. Her passing was an indication that time was short. If Angus and Greg had survived the war, they too would be very old and frail so I needed to find them.

George and I were invited to Joy's funeral and to the home afterwards. Many people read the notice in the paper, attended the funeral and met for tea afterwards.

Iain rang later full of excitement and told me that amongst the mourners was an elderly gentleman who'd served with Maurice at RAF Castletown. The man was called Angus. He only recently discovered that Joy McLennan was his old friend's wife. She had for years been living on another floor in the same home.

Angus's carer only mentioned in passing that Joy had worked in the Castletown NAAFI, and asked if he knew her.

Angus had been well enough to stay for the funeral service, but had left before we could be introduced. Thrilled, I thanked Iain for the new information.

Next Friday, there were three cups of steaming coffee on the desk in the heritage centre when I took my coat off. I glanced around, wondering who else was in with me and George.

He put his hands on my shoulders and pushed me down onto one of the chairs. 'Sit down old girl, there's someone here to see you.'

An elderly white-haired gentleman was wheeled in next to me. He held an old airman's cap which bore a Royal Canadian Airforce badge. My eyes strayed from it to his heavily-wrinkled face. Then the bowed head lifted slowly, revealing a pair of steely, blue eyes.

I could hardly find my voice. 'Were you a Musketeer, or do you know where the others disappeared to when Maurice was killed?'

As he addressed me his eyes welled up. 'I was, and I do. We were immediately reposted on artic convoy cover, pending the investigation. Due to wartime rules, I was gagged by the Official Secrets Act. I did manage to find and send out the photographs Maurice had got printed for us all.

'Joy Chevalier got hers quickly, but your mother had been reposted to Bedford by then. I left it to the mess officer to post one of the photos to her, hoping I'd be able to explain what had happened after the war.'

'Are you my father then? Didn't you know about me?' I asked anxiously.

He leaned a little on the arm of his wheelchair and looked me directly in the eye.

'No, dear, I'm not, but I know who was.'

I hadn't wanted to hear 'was', but I really needed closure.

'We were exonerated. We patrolled in the same squadron for about six months. This was your father's spare dress cap. He was Greg Merrick, twenty three years old and an orphan from Winnipeg. He was mighty struck by your mother. He meant to find her as soon as he could, to explain why he'd left unexpectedly.'

Angus stretched out his hand then and pointed a trembling, bony finger at the light-haired tall airman in Mum's photograph. 'That was your Father and he would have been so proud if he'd known. I'm sorry I cannot give you good news dear.' He lowered his head then and sat for a few minutes as if in respect of his friends.

'Angus, you've given me my life back,' I said. We chatted a while and dipped biscuits in our tea. Then I gave him a heartfelt hug and he left with a carer.

After he'd gone for conformation, George checked on-line once more for airplane crash listings. There he was. RCAF Pilot, Greg Merrick. The report simply stated that his Spitfire was seen downed off Iceland, on October twenty-third, nineteen forty-three, while covering an arctic food convoy. No body was recovered.

I felt sad, but strangely connected to the name on the screen. I was grateful to all the powers that be for the final resolution of my dilemma. Most of all I felt overdue sympathy for Mother, who never knew she was loved by him. I felt emotions surging all over the place then.

A door to my heart had opened. I was ashamed at the anger I'd felt towards my Mother's husband too. After all, he'd loved, cared for and protected me my whole life. He was my Dad.

I went home to grieve for my parents and to heal.

Yesterday, Hamish and I took two wreaths and slipped them into the outgoing tide. I wanted to acknowledge both Maurice's spirit, who I'm sure guided me and my other father, whom I might never had found otherwise.

It seemed a lifetime since I'd asked Dad to send me a sign he was alright. The beach and the weather seemed about the same. The wind still whistled and stung my face, but the haar seemed to be sucking the tributes with it as it withdrew. I promised I would remember all of them, for making me a whole person again, and wished them peace. I was happy.

As Hamish and I made to leave the beach, I sensed an unseen arm around my shoulders. Before I could mention it, there was the unmistakable roar of an aircraft as it emerged from the receding mist. It shot overhead. Then the Spitfire barrel-rolled before veering back out to sea.

We stood in silence for a minute and then raised our eyebrows at each other.

'No-one would believe this, if we told them, but at least we know, eh, Eileen?' Hamish murmured and grinned at me.

Satisfied, we linked arms and headed home.

Mysterious Ways

Jean McLennan

How could a walk with the puppy ever be less fun than a round
of golf? Boring, boring game. Barry could keep it. Ginny's
supercharged tail was always enough to make even a dull day
bright, not that it was needed today. Maybe when she was older
she'd be allowed on the course, but not yet. Golf balls were far
too appealing to a mischievous pup.

In the usual military precision of pre-walk organisation,
gathering poo bags, phone for any emergency, treats, tissues
and if relevant, car keys, I had omitted my seldom-needed sun
glasses and was rueing the oversight. However, it was still
pleasant walking along a narrow country road that twisted
between fields and small copses of trees.

Ginny dived from one interesting clump to another in the
verge, exploring to the furthest extent of her extending lead. A
distant tractor and the occasional chirrup of birds were the only
sounds. I couldn't be completely relaxed, listening for a vehicle,
ready to reel Ginny in and keep her safe, but I was still enjoying
the balmy warmth of the sun on my face.

As we turned a bend in the road an overgrown driveway ran
off to the left. Huge trees suggested grandeur at the end, and I
hesitated for less than a second before deciding to investigate.
Having carried out the usual risk assessment, I unclipped
Ginny's lead and with a joyful yip my pocket rocket took off. A
short distance on, a rotten wooden gate lay almost horizontal
hanging onto the one remaining gatepost with a rusty hinge.
The other post may have been in a state of advanced decay in
some waist high undergrowth on the opposite side, but I barely

noticed its absence as my attention was taken by a white notice, its text illegible, probably due to the elements and passage of time. It remained attached to the centre of the gate.

I can't explain the feeling that washed over me. There, in the warmth of dappled sunshine, a shiver ran down my back. My guts clenched and I felt a sudden, completely unexpected and apparently unwarranted fear. If Ginny hadn't been running ahead, tail swishing, making the decision for me, I would have turned round and carried on down the road. I followed her, dismissing the momentary anxiety as stupid, deliberately taking a deep breath and dropping my shoulders, consciously relaxing.

Avoiding specimen-sized nettles and stones big enough to turn an ankle, I went forward, Ginny running from side to side as if the smells on both sides were equally irresistible. A bend in the drive revealed a huge, red sandstone structure with three rows of windows and a surprisingly small door set in the middle. No grand steps or similar arrangement graced the entrance. Countless chimneys breached the roof. Ginny ran forward and disappeared round one side of the building. I called her back, anxious in case of any unseen hazard.

I spotted a fenced area to the side of the building and decided it would be best to contain her in there for a few minutes, letting her explore to her heart's content. Then we would head back the way we came. Another notice, just legible this time, painted in black paint on wood was nailed to a small gate. Who could object, who would see if I disobeyed the order on it, 'No Dogs Allowed'? The hinge creaked as I pushed it open.

There were no roses, long gone to briar, no plants seeded or rambling out of control without hands to tend them, no seats of wood or stone just knee high undergrowth. A former vegetable garden then.

Ginny dashed to and fro. Suddenly she stopped and scraped at the soil. I felt relief that she wasn't rolling in whatever she'd found. The caravan we were using wasn't the best place to try to remove the stink of fox poo or other doggie delights. I called her in vain, and, beginning to feel uneasy again, I looked down where Ginny was still digging. Earth and the residue of weeds she had dislodged, along with paws going at supersonic speed in her endeavours, made it difficult to see what excited her, but I could see there was something in the bottom of the shallow hole she had created. I decided to bring out the big guns in terms of canine diversions and pulled a ball from my pocket. Ginny's focus changed immediately and I threw it, knowing she would give chase.

I knelt on the ground and brushed soil from the smooth surface emerging below and uncovered a small wooden box. It was the work of several minutes to complete the excavation, time that was punctuated by the need to keep throwing the ball which Ginny hastened to return to me every time, bless her. The wooden box held little interest for her now, but my curiosity was piqued. It was not to be satisfied immediately as a keyhole in the side announced the presence of a lock and, just my luck, the box was locked and the key was absent.

'What's that?' asked Barry nodding towards the box. If he'd had a good round he'd normally regale me with his score and his silence on that topic meant it was probably wise not to ask. When I explained, he picked it up and turned the box over in his hand. It was nicely made and big enough to hold a watch or something similar.

'I think that place was a convent and orphanage years ago. St Maud's Priory it was called. I remember hearing something about the nuns and allegations of cruelty,' he said. Lochenside was where he had spent some of his childhood. Barry's father had been a policeman and had been moved on to different places regularly. Barry had followed his dad into the force and retired four years ago. I'd never been to the area before and it was over fifty years since Barry had been here. He'd often said it held only bad memories for him. Sometimes cop's kids get a rough time from other children, but the well-known golf course was a magnet and the difficulties of his childhood were long past. He'd found one of his old school friends, one that was still single, on Facebook, another golfer, and had set up this holiday. I didn't mind, I had a shopping and theatre trip to London with girlfriends to look forward to in a fortnight's time. And Ginny? As long as she got her walks, playtime and dinner, not necessarily in that order, she was OK wherever we went.

'Can you open it?' I asked.

'Probably,' he replied, taking a bottle of water out of the fridge. 'They could do with a refreshments hut on that course like we have at home.' He took a long drink. I held out the box shaking it under his nose impatient to see its contents, if there were any. Barry sighed, put down the bottle. A tweak with a tiny screwdriver on one of those many gadget knives, the lid fell open and sunlight flashed off the facets of gems. A brooch nestled in folds of purple fabric. The material was in perfect condition as if it had been buried yesterday. I lifted the brooch and turned it over. It was beautiful and looked as if it would be valuable.

'Hand it in as lost property, that's what you should do,' Barry said. I knew that meant we'd probably own it after six months. It would be the easiest course, but...

'I'd rather find out how it came to be there,' I said. 'Who would bury such a thing in a field? And why? It looked like it had been there a long time. The grass and weeds were growing over it. If it hadn't been for Ginny I think no one would ever have found it.'

'Well I suppose no one is going to suddenly spring forth and claim we are stealing it. Go for it then. Where will you start?'

'I'll find out more about St Maud's Priory.' As I placed the brooch back in the box I felt a rustle of something else under its satiny nest. A piece of paper, yellowed and speckled with brown spots, folded over and over to make it as tiny as possible, had been tucked in. Careful not to tear it, I unfolded the sheet to reveal writing. It was in pencil and faint, much of it not legible.

Barry leant over my shoulder and we both tried to make out the message.

'*God forgive me. I need to a..nge Sis.er Ag... ..uelt.   R..er..*'
We looked at each other.
'What does that mean?' we said in unison.
'Sister Agnes? Do you think?' I said.
'Sister Agatha? Your guess is as good as mine.'
'What does this mean?'
Barry shrugged, 'Search me. OK, if it amuses you,' he said, settling down, newspaper in hand, Ginny hastening to rest her chin on his lap, his mind already on other things.

Later that day, when Barry was enjoying his second round, Ginny and I walked from the campsite into the town and as you do, fell into conversation with another dog walker as our dogs cavorted together. Tyler was a Staffie, full of bounce and friendly. Liz, (her appearance might have put others off but in my job as a former social worker I have learned not to prejudge anyone by their appearance) his owner, was at least a whole generation younger than me with piercings adorning her nose, eyebrow, lips and a row of several along the edge of her ears. I didn't like to think where there might be more on her body. She asked if I was on holiday and revealed she was a local. We'd compared notes about our dogs already and exchanged their names before our own.

'What do you know about St Maud's Priory?' I asked. Might as well begin my research now. 'We found it on our walk this morning.'

'What do you want to know? I'm not old enough to remember when it was open, but it was featured on one of those TV programmes about Catholic Church scandals. The nuns were pretty brutal, or at least some of them were, in their so-called care of the orphans. It's been closed down since the nineteen fifties or sixties I think. Most of the children were from single mums. I believe it was a different world back then.'

'Have you any idea how would I find out more?'

'The local priest, lovely chap, Father John, might be able to help. He lives in a cottage right next to the church, down there. It's the one just past the church.' Liz pointed down the main street.

Like Ginny hot on the trail of something, I went immediately in search of Father John. He wasn't hard to find following the directions Liz gave me and when he opened the door he filled the space both in height and width. His hair was thinning, almost leaving a tonsure and he was in mufti except for the ubiquitous white collar. He smiled warmly and welcomed both of us in when I told him I hoped he could help me with some information. Maybe he thought I was a potential convert.

His parlour was part office, part sitting room with furniture that might have served several incumbents in his post before him, but the sofa was comfortable and Ginny settled at my feet having first greeted our host thoroughly. I told him I wanted to know about St Maud's. His face immediately became less friendly and open.

'What do you want to know?' he asked abruptly, looking away. I told him of my find and my wish to find the nun mentioned or an explanation of what the note meant. As I talked he seemed to take a deep breath and relax. His eyebrows rose as I told him about the details of the note, the missing letters. I wondered if I should have deferred my visit till I had the box and its contents with me. When I reached the end of my story Father John stood, hesitated for a moment as if in deep thought. I held my breath wondering if he was going to show me the door given his change of attitude when I first talked about St Maud's, but no, he offered me a cup of tea and a bowl of water, perhaps a biscuit, for Ginny. I accepted. There was no reason to rush back to the caravan. Barry was getting his money's worth for his week-long green fee payment and though there was no refreshment hut, there was a bar and since the sun was, by now at least nearly over the yardarm, he would probably adjourn to it to have a pint with his friend and chew over the shots that didn't quite come up to expectation.

139

'It's sad that the church has come in for so much criticism,' Father John said, nursing his mug of tea. 'So many good things have been done.' He took a sip. 'St Maud's was closed before I came here so I'm not sure what can I tell you.' His hand stroked his face as he spoke.

I'd been trained to spot tells and so I wondered if he was being entirely open. There was another mystery here, maybe.

'Anything that could potentially help,' I prompted.

'Well I don't have a list of the nuns who were there, but you should be able to get that from the National Archives. St Maud's Priory was a Cistercian convent. It means the nuns took a vow of poverty, so a nun shouldn't have a piece of valuable jewellery. Most definitely.'

I couldn't put a finger on why, but there was something about his tone, as if what he was saying meant more to him than just a response to a story he was learning for the first time. Mystery number two was deepening.

'Could it have belonged to an orphan then?' I wondered aloud.

'Most of the children will have come from families with nothing, or very little. Let me know if I can help in any way. I thought at first you were a journalist or something similar when you asked about St Maud's,' the priest said. 'I understand your wanting to solve this mystery.' He broke off eye contact and added, 'Indeed, I am curious about it myself.'

Again I had that strong feeling he knew more than he was saying. I thought about challenging him, but he rose to show us out before I could form words to do so.

'God bless you, my dear and you, too.' He bent to stroke Ginny, who had risen from her snooze and slunk over to solicit more attention as we moved to leave.

I brought Barry up to speed and managed to persuade him to spread the next day's games so there was a gap of time in the middle when he would take care of Ginny and I could go to the local library where there were computers for public use. He wasn't best pleased and reminded me this holiday was for his benefit. I bit my tongue. He followed up with another comment about putting the brooch in lost property. I couldn't pass that one up.

'So when there was an easy way to shelf an investigation...' A difficult case had brought out tenacity in him like an alligator hanging onto its prey. I left the rest hanging; I didn't want him to refuse to take Ginny. We had a loan of the caravan from a friend of a friend on the understanding that the dog was never left alone in it, and I wouldn't abuse that trust.

To placate him, I asked how the afternoon's game had gone and managed to stop my eyes glazing over at the blow by blow, or rather, shot by shot description. I commiserated and congratulated as appropriate. He was in a much better mood by the time our evening meal was ready and even joined us on a short evening walk to show me the police house in which his family had lived during his father's posting.

The National Archive site was easily accessed and there was an entry for St Maud's Priory. It read:-

'*Register and documents held at Lochenside Archive not available at the National Archive.*'

I almost cheered. The information about the function of the building on signage outside said it was the library and local archive. I was in the right place. The librarian pointed to a room in the corner of the library.

'You need to tell me what documents you want to see,' she said. 'Some are white glove. And you must sign a register too.' Moments later I was ensconced in a small room with a large desk and a noisy roof fan, and within ten minutes the woman wheeled in a trolley with all the St Maud's papers.

I easily found a register recording the nun's arrivals into the convent and their dates of death, and quickly established there had been a Sister Agnes from 1943 until the convent closed in

1969. There was no information about where she had gone but she was still alive in 1969. Her family name was in the records too. She had been born Cicely Mary Wakefield. Now to find the author of the note. Was it another nun or an orphan? I checked through the list of nuns there at the same time and could find none with a name that fitted the letters I had – 'R..er..' There was no list of the orphans and a few seconds back at the computer revealed that such records were subject to a one hundred year embargo. I'd hit a brick wall. Time to retrench and think.

I told Barry of my discoveries, but I knew as I spoke he was thinking about his next round on the local course and slightly irritated with me as I'd been a tad longer at the library than he expected. I was explaining about Father John when he butted in, 'Going to try to shave a few shots off yesterday's score. There's just time for me to make the starter by twelve if I go right now. I'll hear your story later.' He gathered up his golf shoes, the clubs were already in the car and he departed muttering, 'Getting to be an obsession.'

I couldn't see how I was going to follow the trail any further. I already knew that adopted children records were available in a very limited way. In spite of the beauty of that afternoon's river walk and the obvious enthusiasm of Ginny, particularly the dashes she made raising ducks, I felt a bit down. Then we met Tyler and Liz again.

I told her the whole story of the brooch and the note.

'Did you find your nun then?' she asked. I shook my head, wrestling a piece of cardboard from Ginny. Tyler was sniffing at it too. 'So where do you go from here?'

'I don't know. I think I've gone as far as I can.'

'If you do find out more, please let me know. I love a mystery.' She told me where she lived and invited me to pop in for a coffee next morning or we could meet on the riverside path and then adjourn for coffee. The arrangement was left like that. I was coming to like Liz. She was easy to talk to and clearly Ginny found Tyler a suitable playmate.

I was surprised to get back to the caravan and find Father John sitting on the step.

'I was thinking whether it would breach the vow of secrecy of confession, but I don't think so.'

My instincts had been right. It wasn't just the possibility of me being a journalist that made him thoughtful. He did know something relevant to the brooch.

'Come in,' I told him. I'm just about to make a cup of tea. You'll join me. My husband is playing golf.' I stumbled up the steps in my haste to get him inside and find out what he knew.

He put out an arm and steadied me. 'Ah, yes. Our famous course. A keen golfer, is he?'

I managed to contain myself, and small talk continued as I bustled about preparing the tea and a plate of biscuits.

'You thought you knew something...'

'Yes. I can't see the harm in telling you. It will be Sister Agnes you are looking for and she still lives here. She is in an old folk's home in town. Her physical health is not good, but her memory is sound as a church bell. I can't see why you might not go and talk to her. You won't upset her, will you?'

'Of course not. If the brooch was hers, she can have it back. I wonder how it came to be where I found it. Thank you for coming and telling me. Do you know anything about the story of her brooch?'

'Nothing that I can tell you,' he said, 'but I think Sister Agnes will.'

Next morning I took Ginny for her usual walk and, turning a bend on the path, saw Liz and Tyler coming towards us. Ginny took off, barking excitedly to greet her canine friend.

'That's great. You can come for coffee now?' Liz asked, her piercings moving disturbingly in her face as she grinned.

'I wonder if I could ask you a favour?' I asked. 'Could you take Ginny for a short time this morning? Maybe up to an hour, no longer? I'm on the trail of Sister Agnes. She's in Sunnyview.'

'You've found her. Excellent.'

I told her about Father John's visit.

'How about going right now? The dogs are fine and you can come straight to my house when you've seen her. I want to know the end of this story.' Ginny and Tyler were looping about in the water. She wasn't even looking, but there was no guarantee what she'd do if I just disappeared, so I called her, clipped on her lead and handed it to Liz.

Sunnyview was a modern, low-rise building set in a small park of mixed trees and grass peppered with a few colourful flower borders. A security system monitored entry and, after a few seconds of waiting for a response to a call button, I was admitted. A badge announced the name and status of the woman who greeted me. Brenda Booth, Manager. I asked to see Sister Agnes.

'Are you a relative?'

'No. I have something I think belongs to her. A brooch.' I paused. 'It was lost some time ago and I think she'll want it back.'

'Wait here. I'll check if she is ready to receive visitors and if she wants to see you. A brooch, eh. What's it like?'

I held it out but not in a way that would allow Brenda to simply take it. I could see she was impressed.

'Looks valuable,' she said.

The first thing I noticed about the bedroom was how light and bright it was. The second was the small, wizened figure slumped in a chair. As I went in, she turned a birdlike head to look. She was unsmiling, severe looking. Without a word she indicated a visitor's chair. Hard plastic, uncomfortable, unlike the one she reposed in.

'Sister Agnes?' I asked. My name is Judi MacGregor. We've never met.' I held out a hand and a thin clawed one responded. It was so frail I hardly dared take even a light grip.

144

I was gathering myself to begin to explain what had happened, but without preamble she went straight to the point.

'My brooch?'

I held it out. She took it in her hand and smiled. Her old face transformed into a pleasant expression. Momentarily, I worried I'd reached the end of the road and would never know the story behind my find. At least I had managed to restore it to its owner. I needn't have worried.

In a tremulous voice she said, 'I never thought to see it again. Roberta, wasn't it? She took it.' I read out the legible parts of the note, which I'd brought with me.

'I understand, lass. She was after revenge. That's what it means.' Sister Agnes stopped for a breath. I waited. 'And she was smart enough to know I couldn't say anything about it as I shouldn't have had the likes of that.'

'Revenge? For what?' I asked. Agnes sighed, ran a clawlike hand over her forehead.

'I shouldn't...I know...it was different times then. I suppose I was jealous, in a way. It's hard to remember why I did what I did.'

I waited, giving her time to think back and catch her breath. After all, this had come out of the blue. She must have thought the brooch was gone forever.

'You see, Roberta and her younger brother, Samuel I think his name was, were being adopted. Their parents had been killed the year before and there was no family to take them so they were at St Maud's.' She stopped gasping, shuddered then took a deep breath. I could hear a rattle in her chest as she did so. If we had taken our holiday next year would she still have been here?

'A couple from Australia were taking them. They were going to a new life.' Her tone, even now, dripped with what sounded like envy. 'Samuel had a toy, a teddy or something like that. It had been his when his parents were alive. He was three when they were being adopted. Roberta was eleven.' Another deep breath and pause, then she went on. 'I don't know now why I

145

took the teddy and told him he couldn't have it. I said it had to stay in St Maud's for the next child. Roberta made a big fuss. Samuel was crying. This happened the day before they were to be collected by the adoptive parents, and there was more fuss when the couple came to take them. It was such a commotion. I told them he didn't want to leave St Maud's and that was why he was upset. They told him of the wonderful things he would have living with them. A dog, a pony, everything. He was crying and didn't really hear what they were saying. They took him off in their car struggling and crying. Roberta just glowered at me. By then she had taken my brooch. I shouldn't have had it at all. The vow of poverty. It should have been sold to help fund God's work. I know that was a sin.'

Father John's mention of confession came to me and a penny dropped.

'So she, Roberta, buried it with the note?'

'She must have. Where you found it. I'll never know how she knew about it. The brooch had been my grandmother's. It was all I had of my family when I took holy orders. I had a child out of marriage. That was my first sin. A boy, a beautiful boy he was, but still-born. My family cut me off. Except my grandmother. She gave that to me on her deathbed when I was twelve. I cherished it. I had no way of living but I wouldn't sell the brooch. I was only fourteen when I had the baby. The sin, my second, keeping the brooch, lay heavily on me, but I just couldn't give it up. I didn't tell a soul, but God saw. He took it from me as a punishment.'

I couldn't help what I said next. 'And did you not see that to the little boy, Samuel, the teddy was the same thing? It was all he had of his parents.'

I was rewarded for this comment with a hard look.

Sister Agnes gazed at the brooch, turning it in her hand, then looked out of the window with unseeing eyes. I was sure she was picturing events of almost sixty years ago.

'He got his teddy. Before they left for Australia, his adoptive father came back to St Maud's and demanded to have the thing.

He was livid, I remember. As I said, in those days things were different in this country at least. Children were to be seen and not heard, spare the rod and spoil the child.'

I left shortly after. I found her remarks, her excuse for what she did, hard to swallow. She had not had a happy time herself but that wasn't a good excuse. The mystery was solved, but somehow the whole saga made me feel sad. She had no regret for her actions. Her own selfish perception of the whole thing was paramount. Had she been as insensitive to all the children in her care? I hoped not.

Friday was the last day of our holiday and once again Father John surprised me at our caravan as I returned from walking Ginny, who greeted him as an old friend.

'I hoped to catch you before you left. I thought you should know that Sister Agnes has given her brooch to me to sell with the instruction the money raised should be shared among the children in the nearest Barnardo's home, specifying they are to be allowed to choose a toy for themselves with their share. She seems more at peace with herself now. Bless you for spending so much of your holiday on this mission.'

I didn't ask what he had known when I first met him. It wasn't relevant now. Perhaps he only now knew the story of Sam and Roberta. Perhaps, sadly, it was a story among many similar ones. I thanked him for taking the trouble to come to tell me.

I wondered if what I said to Sister Agnes had made the difference. I would never know, but now the whole story had somehow acquired a happy ending. When I told Liz of the latest development, I was surprised at her comment, 'God works in mysterious ways.'

Read more by Jean.
http://www.jeanmclennan.co.uk

Printed in Poland
by Amazon Fulfillment
Poland Sp. z o.o., Wrocław